3I

JM
GS

This book must be returned by the date specified at the time of issue as the DATE DUE FOR RETURN.
The loan may be extended (personally, by post, telephone or online) for a further period if the book is not required by another reader, by quoting the above number / author / title.

Enquiries: 01709 336774

www.rotherham.gov.uk/libraries

'Molly? Are you sure?'

'That I want to kiss you?' She closed her eyes, her body leaning slightly towards him. 'That I want you to kiss me back?' She looked at him, desperation, need and longing in her tone. 'Oh, yes, Fletcher. I want that. I need that—right now.'

Her last two words were soft, and accompanied by an irresistible sensual tremor.

No man in his right mind could fight the temptation any longer, and with one swift move he slipped his arms about her, drawing her close, before lowering his head to capture her lips in a kiss so intensely powerful he felt as though the earth had literally shifted beneath them.

Dear Reader,

Here is the final story in the Wilton triplets series. Like her other two sisters, Molly has her own unique personality—and it was great to finally let her shine bright. Doing her last year in a busy hospital as a surgical registrar means she's bound by strict time constraints, and yet taking part in hospital events such as Clown Patrol brings her a lot of delight. We see her working late, studying and trying to come to terms with her emotional past, and it really lets us see the inner workings of vivacious Molly.

These aspects are clearly what draw Fletcher to her in the first place, and although they haven't seen each other for such a long time it's clear from the get-go that their underlying attraction is still very much alive.

Many times when I'm writing a character he or she often reveals aspects of personality that I hadn't originally thought of. This is fantastic for a writer, because it means that the character is 'coming alive', so I was not only surprised but excited to discover that Fletcher was a magician! Of course he has a lot of other skills, but this fun-loving side of his personality, as well as his drive to help those less fortunate than him, are attributes that not only attracted Molly in the past but also attract her in the present.

I really enjoyed helping Molly and Fletcher to achieve their happy ending, and my Epilogue finalises the stories of the Wilton triplets. However, stay tuned—because Stacey, Cora and Molly's younger sister Jasmine is already starting to 'come alive'!

With warmest regards

Lucy

STILL MARRIED TO HER EX!

BY
LUCY CLARK

First published in Great Britain 2015
by Mills & Boon, an imprint of Harlequin (UK) Limited.
Large Print edition 2015
Eton House, 18-24 Paradise Road,
Richmond, Surrey, TW9 1SR

© 2015 Anne Clark & Peter Clark

ISBN: 978-0-263-25521-8

Harlequin (UK) Limited's policy is to use papers that
are natural, renewable and recyclable products and made
from wood grown in sustainable forests. The logging
and manufacturing processes conform to the legal
environmental regulations of the country of origin.

Printed and bound in Great Britain
by CPI Antony Rowe, Chippenham, Wiltshire

Lucy Clark is actually a husband-and-wife writing team. They enjoy taking holidays with their children, during which they discuss and develop new ideas for their books using the fantastic Australian scenery. They use their daily walks to talk over the characterisation and fine details of the wonderful stories they produce, and are avid movie buffs. They live on the edge of a popular wine district in South Australia with their two children, and enjoy spending family time together at weekends.

Books by Lucy Clark

Mills & Boon Medical Romance

A Child to Bind Them
Dr Perfect on Her Doorstep
Her Mistletoe Wish
The Secret Between Them
Resisting the New Doc in Town
One Life-Changing Moment
Dare She Dream of Forever?
Falling for Dr Fearless
Diamond Ring for the Ice Queen
Taming the Lone Doc's Heart
The Boss She Can't Resist
Wedding on the Baby Ward

Visit the Author Profile page
at millsandboon.co.uk for more titles.

To the amazing, wonderful and talented
Liz Bentley. I cannot thank you enough for
the educational support you have provided
to my children over the years, especially
2014. You impact your students in the most
positive way and make them feel proud of their
accomplishments. You are a brilliant teacher.
Many, many thanks.

Romans 14:8

**Praise for
Lucy Clark**

'A sweet and fun romance about second
chances and second love.'

—*HarlequinJunkie* on
Dare She Dream of Forever?

CHAPTER ONE

MOLLY FINISHED APPLYING the last of the face paint, grinned at herself in the mirror and turned to head back to her locker situated in the surgical theatre changing rooms. This was one of the highlights of her job as a surgical registrar— being rostered on with other registrars to take part in the clown patrol through the paediatric ward. All departments were involved and the fun times they had helped with inter-department bonding.

Today she was rostered on with her fellow surgical registrar, Alexis, and two others from the urology department. It didn't matter that she'd been in Theatre all night long or that she had a lecture to attend this afternoon. It didn't matter that prior to her entering the changing rooms, her eyes were scratchy, her feet tired and her mind had almost turned to mush.

'It's the happiness on the faces of those kids

that matters,' she said out loud, her spirits lifting as she looked down at her brightly coloured jumpsuit. She pulled her blonde curly hair back into a flat bun and added some clips to keep the flyaway wisps in place. Ever since she'd moved from Newcastle to Sydney in order to complete her surgical training, her bouncy waves had turned into unruly curls thanks to the mix of humidity and drizzle.

'Sorry, sorry, sorry.' Alexis panted as she came rushing through the door, rainbow-coloured curly wigs in her hands. 'The lift was packed so I raced up the five flights and—'

Molly waved away her friend's explanation as she took the wigs. 'No drama. Sit down and catch your breath while I fix your wig in place.' Alexis did as she was bid but within a second, Molly gasped. 'Did you get the noses?'

'Right here.' Alexis pulled them from her pocket.

'Excellent.' Molly pinned Alexis's wig in place then tended to her own before accepting the squishy red clown nose, which actually honked, and sliding it onto her own. She squeezed it twice, the two women laughing at the noise it made. 'All ready to entertain the troops.'

'We'd better get moving. They were expecting us at least half an hour ago.' She picked up their bag of tricks as they exited the changing rooms.

'It's not really our fault that morning theatre ran late.' Molly shrugged her shoulders. 'But at least Mr Derriack is now on the mend and doing well in Recovery.'

The two women continued to chat as they headed quickly along the corridor, then down three flights of stairs. 'We are so late,' Alexis remarked again as they finally arrived at the paediatric ward. 'Here's hoping the urology boys have been holding down the fort.'

Molly opened the door and they both slipped inside, their bag of balloons and funny tricks at their side all ready to entertain the children.

'There you are,' Taylor, the paediatric sister, said as they came in the door.

'Theatre ran late,' Alexis offered as they headed to the children's playroom where many of the small patients had gathered. For those who were still bedridden or too sick to join in the fun in the playroom, Molly and Alexis would pay them a special visit, hopefully bringing a smile to their sad little faces.

'At least you're here,' Taylor added.

'Why? Where are the urology registrars?' Alexis asked.

'Held up in Theatre, but, thankfully, a visiting research surgeon was chatting with the ward clerk and he said he could do magic tricks. And he can.' Taylor pointed to where a man was busy entertaining a group of children, all of them totally captivated by his performance. 'He came right over and saved the day.' Taylor's eyes were wide with delight. 'He's been entertaining the kids for the past fifteen minutes.'

'Wow. A doctor who can do magic. I like him already.' Molly laughed as they took a peek around the corner of the playroom. The children sitting there were staring at the doctor with such rapt attention, his white coat having been removed, his blue shirt sleeves rolled up as he magically pulled row after row of brightly coloured handkerchiefs from his closed fist.

Molly's real smile vanished as she stared at the magic doctor, her heart skipping at least two beats. 'Fletch!' The name was whispered in shock, her body starting to get in on the act by trembling. What in the world was he doing here? At her hospital? In the paediatric ward? Doing magic tricks?

'Ready, Molly?' Alexis was clapping as the magic doctor finished pulling a string of colourful handkerchiefs out of his closed fist with an expert flourish. 'Molly?' Alexis asked a moment later, looking closely at her friend. 'What's wrong? You're whiter than the face paint.'

'Uh…' Molly turned her head, not wanting to look at the man who had once set her heart to racing, who had made her entire body tremble with desire, who had stolen her heart.

'Are you sick?' Alexis rested her hand on Molly's shoulders and looked into her eyes. 'Taylor's gone to thank the magic doctor and introduce us.' Alexis stared at her for another moment before saying, 'I'm glad you've got a painted smile on your face otherwise you'd be the most frightened clown I've ever seen.'

Molly glanced once more in Fletcher's direction. Why was he here? At Sydney General? She tried to think clearly and recalled Taylor saying that he was one of the visiting research surgeons.

How was Fletcher Thompson a visiting research surgeon? He was supposed to be overseas, saving the world. At least, that was where he'd been the last time she'd had any sort of contact with him.

'Molly? Come on,' Alexis implored. 'I really need you to pull it together. Taylor's introducing us.'

Eyes widening, Molly hoped Taylor wouldn't say her name, but then she remembered that she wasn't being introduced as Molly Wilton, Senior Surgical Registrar. No. She was in disguise. She was 'Moppet' and Alexis was 'Squeaky'. Perhaps that might mean that Fletcher would have no clue who she was. It was possible.

Molly straightened her shoulders and cleared her throat, nodding to Alexis. 'I'm ready. How about you, Squeaky?'

Alexis replied in a falsetto voice. 'Ready to have supery-doopery, fun-funny-fun.'

Molly managed a true smile just as Taylor finished introducing them. All the children turned to look in their direction with eager expressions on their faces. Together, the two clowns skipped to the front where the children were gathered,

Molly doing her level best to ignore the 'magic doctor'.

Where she'd half expected Fletcher to leave once she and Alexis started their routine, he didn't. He stayed and laughed and clapped along with the children. Even after the show was over, Molly and Alexis heading to the wards to spend some time with the less mobile children, she was still highly aware that Fletcher was on the ward, hanging around. Had he recognised her beneath her face paint and silly clown clothes? He wasn't watching her all the time, wasn't trying to talk to her alone, wasn't even in the same room as her. How could he possibly know?

They hadn't had any contact for the past fourteen years, ever since she'd signed the divorce papers. Too young to know better, too young to be married. She'd always thought she'd never see him again but now here he was, at *her* hospital. Why? Was it just a coincidence?

'Moppet? Moppet?'

A small five-year-old girl was tugging on Molly's brightly coloured clown costume, demanding her attention. Molly honked her clown nose, making the little girl giggle. It was best she continued to forget that Fletcher Thompson was even in the building…at least for now.

She and Alexis made balloon animals and told funny jokes and when the urology registrars finally arrived, they did a little slapstick skit that involved a lot of falling down and silly noises.

'And…we're done!' Alexis sighed almost two hours later as they left the paediatric ward. She pulled off her colourful wig as they made their way back to the theatre changing rooms. 'Woo-ee, this thing makes me hot and sweaty. Doesn't it make you hot, Molly? And your hair is so much longer and curlier than mine.' Alexis fluffed her fingers through her short, spiky brown locks.

Molly walked briskly along the corridor just wanting to return to the changing rooms as soon as possible, for there was no way she wanted to risk bumping into Fletcher. 'If I cut my hair short and coloured it like a rainbow, I wouldn't even need to wear the wig,' she responded absent-mindedly.

'That might be fun to see,' a deep voice said from just behind them. She didn't need to turn around to see who had spoken. Nor did she need

Alexis stopping in the middle of the corridor and smiling at the man who was brilliant at magic tricks.

'I once knew a woman who had blonde curls that used to go really tight when it was humid. Do yours do that?' The rich timbre of his deep voice washed over her, creating a long-repressed sensation of awareness. Why had he come here? Why was he forcing her boxed-up memories to return to the surface?

Alexis stopped walking and turned to face him. 'Hey there, magic man. Excellent tricks. The kids loved them.'

'Thanks.' He proffered his hand and Alexis quickly shook it. 'Fletcher Thompson.'

'Alexis Borello.'

Molly had wanted to keep walking down the corridor, to get back to the changing rooms as quickly as possible so that she didn't have to face Fletcher, not yet. She wanted more time to figure out what he was doing here and whether he knew who she really was.

'This is my colleague,' Alexis was saying, gesturing to Molly.

'Uh…I think that's my phone,' Molly interrupted, her voice a little louder, a little more frantic, a little more panicked than usual. She reached into her clown bag and pulled out the hospital portable phone that all doctors who were on call had to carry. Unfortunately for her, the phone had become entangled with several left-over balloons and glitter sticks, a few of them falling to the floor. Molly didn't care. She started to walk as she checked the phone. 'Darn. Missed a call. Gotta go.'

Not caring whether she left Alexis behind or not, Molly all but sprinted up the corridor, startling a few people when she rounded the corner near theatres because it wasn't every day you saw a frantic clown dashing towards the theatre block.

Even once she was safe inside the female changing rooms, Molly's heart rate didn't return to normal. Fletch was here. Fletcher was here. *Her* Fletch was here, in the hospital! What was she supposed to do? Being that close to him, smelling his glorious scent, remembering the way his clever, ingenious hands had touched and tickled and tantalised.

'Stop it,' she told herself as she stood in front of the mirror, wiping off the clown make-up. Her hair was now free from the wig and she was dressed in her own comfortable jeans and T-shirt. 'Whatever you had with him is in the past. You both tried to make it, you both failed,' she continued to remind her reflection. 'It's over.' So why did her body feel more alive than it had in years? Just the sight of Fletcher was enough to make her tingle all over. Closing her eyes, she hung her head. Why couldn't she get the man out of her system?

'Because he's Fletch,' she whispered.

'What is up with you?' Alexis came into the changing rooms, enunciating every word slowly and individually. Molly jumped, startled at her friend's appearance. 'You fair bolted away from the nice visiting magician doctor man.' Her friend tut-tutted. 'It's not like you to run from a handsome, incredibly clever man, so what gives? Was it his brilliant magic tricks or the way he smiled that scared you more?'

Molly looked at her friend in the mirror before turning to face her. Shoulders back, chin jutting out with defiance, she opened her mouth, her tone haughty. 'I didn't appreciate his comments about my hair. They were far too…familiar.'

Alexis stared at her for a moment, completely baffled. 'Really? I'm sure he didn't mean anything by it. He was probably just trying to be friendly.'

Molly frowned and slumped her shoulders. It wasn't fair for her to take her annoyance with Fletch out on her friend. 'I'm sorry, Alexis. I guess I'm just overly tired.'

'Well, you were in emergency theatres half the night and then elective theatres all morning. You deserve at least a little bit of rest.'

Molly nodded. 'I think I'll head home and catch some sleep before the lecture this afternoon.'

Alexis was still looking at her with such concern and confusion, Molly didn't blame her. 'All right. I might head to the residential wing and do the same. Entertaining children does tend to make a person rather tired.' She chuckled and stepped forward to give Molly a hug. 'Go and sleep. I'll take care of packing up the clown things.'

'Really?' Molly tried unsuccessfully to smother a yawn. 'Thanks, that would be great.'

Alexis agreed that she was indeed 'great' and, with a laugh, Molly grabbed her bag from her locker and headed out of the changing rooms, calling goodbye to some of the theatre staff before she reached the main corridor.

It was there that she saw him. There that she stopped. There that she stared.

'Hello, Molly.' He was leaning against the wall on the opposite side of the doors that lead to the theatre department. So casual. So relaxed. So... gorgeous.

'Fletcher.'

His smile was natural, wide, hypnotic and she had a difficult time not being affected by it. Why did he have to be even more handsome than when they'd first met? His hair was still dark, still wavy, the only change being a little bit of grey on the sides near his ears. His shoulders were still broad and she quickly clutched her suddenly itchy fingers together in an effort to stop herself from reaching out and touching the perfectly sculptured abdominals that she knew were hiding beneath his blue shirt.

However it was his eyes, his wonderful blue eyes that had melted her heart on so many different occasions, that now seemed to connect with her soul, reuniting them in a way she'd never even known existed.

'You seem surprised to see me,' he said.

'I…er…am. How are you?'

'Stunned that you didn't even compliment me on my magic tricks.' Fletch held his arms out wide as he walked towards her. 'Not even a hug?'

'Fletcher.' She put her hands up to stop him. 'Don't.' He dropped his arms back to his sides but she realised he was standing closer now than before and the scent of spicy yumminess, the scent she'd always equated with him, surrounded her. Molly closed her eyes for a second, fighting the overwhelming urge to throw her arms around his neck and press her lips to his. This was Fletch. *Her* Fletcher. She'd never thought she'd ever see him again, especially after what they'd endured together, but here he was, right in front of her, looking even more wonderful than before. She swallowed and opened her eyes, determined to gain control over her mind and traitorous body.

'Don't what?'

Molly fixed him with a glare, clearly noting that twinkle in his eyes. He'd always been such a larrikin, a delightful teaser, an expert flirter. She didn't want to flirt with him. No. She was seeing Roger and, for all she knew, Fletch could have a wife tucked away somewhere. In short, she knew nothing about his present situation and she wasn't sure she wanted to. He was her past, not her present. 'Do the old long-lost-friends greeting thing.'

'But we are old friends and when I see old friends, I give them a hello hug.' He paused for a second before continuing. 'Or…we could just nod politely at each other instead.' He nodded his head once in greeting then shrugged one shoulder as though he didn't really care one way or the other.

He was doing it again. He was twisting her thoughts, making her flustered, causing her heart rate to increase, her breathing to become shallow, her knees to go weak. Why was he still so handsome? Why were the sensations she'd thought blissfully dormant now surging to life, zinging around her body as though humming a happy tune?

'I thought you were a magnificent clown,' he stated, when she didn't say anything.

Molly stared at him for a second, a little perplexed. 'You knew it was me?'

Fletch's warm chuckle washed over her, soothing her like a warm blanket. She'd forgotten just how wonderful that sound was. 'I'd know you anywhere, Molly.' He leaned against the wall, his tone sincere. 'How have you been?'

She frowned, opened her mouth to reply, then closed it again and shook her head. She moved away from him, needing distance. 'I can't do this, Fletcher.'

'Do what? Talk to an old friend?'

'We're not friends, Fletch.' There was a hint of warning in her tone. Seeing him again had turned her mind to mush, had brought back all those old memories, those old feelings, those old hurts. She couldn't remember another time in her life, except with the death of her parents, when she'd been more devastated and miserable than when she and Fletcher had parted ways.

'We're not?' He seemed surprised by this and she wasn't sure why. Didn't he remember how things had ended between them? What he'd said to her all those years ago?

'Look…I just…I can't.' With that, Molly turned on her heel and all but sprinted towards the stairwell, praying he wouldn't follow her. She stalked through the hospital, hearing someone call her name but not stopping to see who it was. She just needed to get home, to a place of sanctuary. She needed to sort out her thoughts but most of all she needed to breathe properly as the pains in her chest were starting to squeeze her.

She shouldn't be surprised that they'd returned. The only other time she could remember having bad anxiety pains was when she'd been arguing with Fletcher. She hadn't been able to fathom how someone she loved so much could exasperate her even more. It was ridiculous. She could work for over twenty-four hours and still concentrate. She could help raise her siblings, dealing with all sorts of problems. She could even perform difficult surgical procedures and throughout all of these usually stressful situations she'd never once experienced the anxiety pains she had when she was around Fletcher.

'Time to call for reinforcements.' As she walked she pulled her cell phone from her bag and instantly called the first number on her speed dial. 'Stace. It's me,' she said as soon as her sister answered the call. It was great that she could always count on her family for support. Being one

of three, even though she was the youngest triplet, meant she'd never been alone and that bond,
the one she shared with Stacey and Cora, made
her happy, especially when she needed them—
like now.

'Hi. I'm just about to call in my next patient.
Busy clinic,' Stacey offered. 'Can I call you—?'

'Fletcher's here.' Molly's words tumbled out in
a rush. 'In Sydney. At the hospital. I've just seen
him. Just spoken to him.'

Stacey gasped at this news. 'OK. Um…where
are you?'

'I'm walking home.'

'Right. I'll call you in five minutes.'

'Get Cora.'

'I was going to.' There was love and support
radiating in her sister's tone and when Molly disconnected the call, she was able to drag in a deep
and calming breath. 'Thank goodness for sisters,'
she muttered as she tossed her phone back into
her bag and took out her house keys. The hospital owned several cottage and duplex proper-
ties close by, making them available for medical
staff to rent.

Molly had been fortunate to complete the majority of her surgical rotation in Newcastle, close to her siblings, but, to finish her training, a move to Sydney had been imperative. For her final year of surgical rotation, she'd been able to secure a placement in Sydney, which was only a short two-hour drive from Newcastle. Now that her sister Cora and her husband, Archer, along with their adopted son Nee-Ty, or Ty, for short, were also in Newcastle, providing further family support, Molly hadn't felt so bad in shifting to Sydney.

The small ground-floor duplex cottage she'd been able to rent was exactly what she'd needed. Two bedrooms, one bathroom and plenty of room for her to lounge around and watch old black-and-white movies to help unwind from the busy bustling of the hospital. Since she'd been living here, the other half of the duplex next door had only been rented on a short-term basis, several visiting surgeons, professors and nurses staying there, most of them keeping to themselves and not bothering her.

Usually, she found her little place quite relaxing, but now all she could do was to pace around, cell phone in hand, waiting impatiently for her sisters to call her back. When her phone rang, Molly instantly connected the call.

'What am I supposed to do?' she wailed without even bothering to say hello.

'Oh, Molly.' Cora's tone was filled with empathy. 'I feel your anxiety.'

'So how did he look?' Stacey, the sensible triplet, asked, her voice echoing a bit due to the call being on speaker phone. Molly had always been able to rely on Stacey to get her thinking more logically but at the moment she wasn't sure it was going to work.

'He looks...*so good*.' Molly breathed the last two words. 'But what could I expect? He's Fletcher. He's always been devastatingly handsome and now he's even more distinguished and gorgeous.'

'Why is he there? Is it a permanent move?' Again Stacey came back with the solid questions.

'I might be able to come to Sydney for a few days,' Cora added. 'I can get Archer to cover my clinics.'

At the support she was receiving from her sisters, she started to calm down. Her initial anxiety and stress over seeing Fletch, of talking to him, was starting to wane. Perspective. All she needed right now was a bit of perspective. Cora's offer to drop everything to come and be with her helped Molly realise that her situation wasn't really that dire.

'No. I should be fine. Even just talking to the two of you on the phone is helping me to calm down.'

'That's what we're here for,' Cora added.

'So you don't know why he's at the hospital?' Stacey's question was a good one.

'The paediatric sister said he was a visiting research doctor. Not sure in what discipline but—' Molly stopped talking as her brain started working.

'What is it?' Stacey asked.

'I have to attend a lecture this afternoon.' Molly sighed heavily.

'I didn't think you had lectures today.' Cora always knew her schedule off by heart. It was that amazing memory her triplet had and as Molly was about to sit her final exams, she wished she'd been the triplet to get the almost photographic memory.

'It's a special one as a visiting researcher has

arrived at the hospital and is generously sharing his knowledge with us. Alexis told me about it, said it would be important to attend as some of the techniques he'll be talking about may appear in our final surgical examinations.'

'And you think this visiting researcher is Fletcher?' Cora's tone held intrigue. 'I wonder what the lecture's on.'

'That's not the point, sis.'

'Do you really think it's Fletcher? He might be there for another reason,' Stacey added.

'Ha.' Molly laughed without humour. 'Of course he'll be the one delivering the lecture. It would be just my luck not to be able to avoid him while he's at Sydney General.'

'Wait a second,' Stacey said. 'Did he know you worked there?'

Molly frowned for a moment, considering her sister's question. 'I don't know. He didn't seem surprised to see me. At least, I don't think he did. Remember, the first time I saw him I was dressed as Moppet the clown.'

'Well, as a *visiting* doctor, at least it means he'll only be there for a short while.'

'Good point, Stace.' Molly was happy with this information.

'You only need to hang on, keep your emotions under control and then he'll be gone again,' Stacey continued.

'And we're here to help you cope with any repercussions from bumping into him,' Cora continued.

'And you only need to see him at the hospital and you have clinics and operating sessions and emergencies to help you avoid him as much as possible.'

'And we get to talk everything through any time you need.'

Her sisters' words tumbled over each other and again Molly found she was able to let go of her tension. Deep breaths were easy now, the pain in her chest completely gone. 'You're both right. I can do this. It's only for a short while and I'll be home with you all on the weekend.'

'You can do it, sis.' Cora's tone was filled with determination.

'I only need to see him at the hospital.' There was a knock at Molly's front door. 'I can do this,' she reiterated to her sisters. 'Hang on a moment, there's someone at my door.'

With phone in hand, feeling more relaxed and calm, Molly opened her front door—only to come face to face with Fletcher Thompson once more.

'Molly!'

'Fletcher!'

'You live here.' It was a statement, not a question.

'Yes.' She glared at him. 'Did you follow me home?'

'What? No!' His denial was instant and as she glanced at him, still dressed in the same suit he'd been wearing at the hospital, it was only then she also realised he had a suitcase beside him and a set of keys in his hand. He pointed to the second duplex cottage. 'I'm…er…supposed to be staying there for the next two weeks.'

He reached into his jacket pocket for a piece of paper and showed it to her as though needing to prove that he wasn't stalking her. With her mind whirring, her body zinging to life due to his nearness and her annoyance rising, she all but snatched the paper from his hand and quickly read it.

Sure enough, it stated that Dr Fletcher Thompson, MBBS, PhD, Fellow of the Royal Australasian College of Surgeons, Visiting Research Fellow, was staying next door for a two-week period.

Molly dropped her hand back to her side and stared at him in shock. 'It's true. You're living next door to me.' Then, to her chagrin, a slow, small smile spread across Fletcher's gorgeous lips, his hypnotic eyes alive with delight, his eyebrows wiggling up and down in a teasing and friendly manner.

'Howdy, neighbour.' He winked. 'Mind if I borrow a cup of sugar?'

CHAPTER TWO

MOLLY HAD BEEN so shocked at this new turn of events she'd simply closed the door in his face, trying not to be affected by his deep chuckle. She put the phone back to her ear and stalked to the farthest part of her house away from the connecting wall, her anxiety back in full swing.

Cora and Stacey did their best to calm her down yet again but Molly now felt like a caged animal. She'd been so tired, so drained before but now it was as though she were living on pure adrenaline and it was powered by anxiety. Not the best thing when she needed to concentrate on the upcoming lecture—a lecture she was now positive Fletcher was giving. Soon she would be a qualified general surgeon but not if she couldn't get her mind in gear.

She'd been taught how to pigeonhole her thoughts, how to concentrate solely on the patient and to push everything else aside. She needed to do that now. She needed to pigeon-hole Fletch Thompson, the man who had once been the love of her life, and focus on whatever Fletcher Thompson, brilliant surgeon and visiting speaker, had to say.

Instead of staying home and trying not to listen for sounds of Fletch moving around next door, Molly headed back to the hospital. If she wasn't going to be able to rest, she'd at least focus her thoughts on something practical. She had a mountain of paperwork to get through and patients to review.

She sat in the little office she shared with Alexis, dictating letters. When Alexis walked in a while later, she was surprised to find her there.

'I thought you were at home,' Alexis said.

'Mind's too busy.'

'Hmm.' Alexis nodded thoughtfully and sat down at her messy desk. 'Does it have anything to do with the lecture Fletcher Thompson is giving?'

Molly turned and stared at her friend. 'So he *is* giving it.' She sighed with resignation, a part of her having still hoped she'd grasped the wrong end of the stick. 'How? Why? Why is he even here? How did it happen?'

Alexis grinned at her. 'You really are in a tizz about him, aren't you?'

'Just…answer the questions. Please?'

Alexis shrugged one shoulder and picked up the top set of case notes from the huge pile on her desk. 'All I know is that last week, the CEO contacted the department, said a visiting research fellow was willing to add Sydney General hospital to the end of his touring schedule and that he'd arrive this week. He'll be giving a series of lectures as well as hands-on theatre demonstrations over the next two weeks.' Alexis looked at her with concern. 'Molly? What's going on?'

At Alexis's words, Molly dragged in a deep breath and let it out slowly as she opened her eyes. Focus on work. That was what she had to do. 'Do we know what he's demonstrating? Is it a new technique?'

Alexis gave her a quizzical look but thankfully didn't probe further. 'Could be both. I guess we'll have to go and find out.'

Molly smiled absently. 'It'd just be like Fletch to invent something that helps others.'

'Fletch?' Alexis raised both eyebrows with great interest and it was only then Molly even realised she'd spoken her thoughts out loud. 'What's going on here? You're as jittery as a long-tailed cat in a room full of rocking chairs. Clearly you know the great and powerful Fletcher. What gives?'

Molly clutched her hands together, looking down at the ground before raising her gaze to meet her friend's. 'I can't…talk about it, Lexi.' She shook her head slowly. 'Not now.'

Alexis continued to stare at her for a moment, concern in her eyes. 'Fair enough. Besides, we both need to concentrate.' Alexis opened their office door and as they stepped out into the corridor she put a reassuring hand on Molly's shoulder. 'Want to slip in at the back of the lecture theatre? That way you won't run the risk of bumping into him again.'

Molly sighed with relief and hugged her friend. 'Thank you.'

Alexis smiled and the two of them headed off to the large hospital lecture theatre. Molly was pleased that the lights had just dimmed as they slipped into the lecture theatre, the slide presentation about to start. Even though Fletcher was standing down at the front, illuminated by the light near the lectern, she hoped that if she concentrated just on the slides and not on his handsome face or sultry voice, then she'd have some chance of remembering what was being presented.

It didn't take long for her to recollect what a genius the man was. When they'd met, he'd just finished medical school and had had plans not only to study surgery but to dedicate his life to working in Third World countries, of helping those less fortunate than himself, of participating in scientific breakthroughs and, if necessary, inventing new equipment to deal with whatever needed to be done. It was one of the reasons why, when they'd parted, she'd known it was the right thing to do. Yes, they'd had a connection, yes, they'd been impulsive and yes, they'd shared a tragedy but as far as Molly had been concerned, they'd both wanted different things for the future and there was no way she was going to be cited as the reason why Fletcher hadn't achieved his dreams.

She'd been only eighteen when they'd met and almost twenty-one the last time she'd seen him…

before today. Now, at thirty-four, she was not the same impulsive innocent. Sure, she liked to go out dancing and, yes, she was definitely a people person, but if there was one thing tragedy had taught her it was to enjoy life to the best of her ability while still keeping sight of what was important.

Family was important. Career was important. Health was important and she felt she'd achieved an excellent balance of those things as well as still having fun with her friends. Impulsive decisions were kept to small things, such as choosing to buy a new jacket or a pair of boots, not running off to Las Vegas and—

'So if we could have the lights back on, please?' Fletcher's words interrupted her thoughts and she realised she'd actually missed the last few minutes of his presentation. Light flooded the lecture theatre and Molly blinked as her eyes adjusted. She'd have to ask Alexis if she could borrow her notes. Annoyed with herself for not paying better attention, she shifted in her chair.

'Ah, yes—thank you for volunteering.' Fletcher was holding out his arm towards her. Molly looked around. What had she missed? Had he said something after he'd asked for the lights to be turned on? Several of her colleagues were staring at her, some with looks of pure envy. What? What was going on?

'Yes, Dr...Wilton, is it? I'd appreciate your assistance down the front as I demonstrate exactly how the device works. You'll also be assisting me in Theatre tomorrow afternoon when we'll be demonstrating the full procedure.'

As he spoke her name Molly's annoyance increased but this time she wasn't annoyed with herself but with Fletcher. Why was he tormenting her like this? Wasn't it bad enough that she had to live next door to him, see him at the hospital and listen to his lectures? Why did he feel the need to torture her in front of her colleagues as well?

She stood up from her seat and made her way to the front of the lecture room as two of the interns set up a mannequin for demonstration purposes. She was aware of Fletcher talking to the room full of people, of explaining more about the procedure and how tomorrow's surgery would highlight even more facets of the invention.

As part of her training, it was an honour she'd

been chosen and she knew several of her colleagues were presently green with jealousy but all
she could focus on was getting through the next
ten or so minutes standing close to Fletcher. She
was aware of his scent, of the warmth exuding
from his close proximity and when their fingers
touched as he repositioned where she was holding the retractor, the tingles that shot up her arm
exploded throughout the rest of her body.

She tried not to gasp at the touch, highly conscious that Fletcher was wearing a microphone
headset so the rest of the room could hear what
he was saying. She didn't want her idiocy to be
picked up by the device and broadcast to everyone gathered here. Why had he chosen her?
Molly closed her eyes for a second, needing to
gather her wits, to think logically like Stacey,
to be concerned for what she was learning like
Cora.

'And generally,' Fletch said into the microphone, 'it is advisable to keep your eyes open
throughout the entire procedure.'

Molly's eyelids snapped open and she glared at
him. There was a twinkle in his eyes and a small
teasing grin twitching at the corner of his mouth.

'Something I'm positive Dr Wilton will employ tomorrow when we're actually in Theatre.' He delivered the words without chastisement and filled with humour, garnering a smattering of laughter from the gathered audience.

The rest of the demonstration proceeded without incident, Molly determined to be one hundred per cent professional, not caring in the slightest that Fletch was so near to her. Finally, after thanking her for her time and assistance, Fletcher ended the lecture. Thankfully, he was immediately swamped with several people coming up to talk to him, to ask him further questions, and Molly was able to leave. She stalked briskly down the corridor, intent on heading home, getting some sleep and doing her best to put Fletcher Thompson right out of her mind.

It wasn't going to be easy, especially with him prowling around next door, but she could lock her doors and windows and hibernate in her bedroom listening to loud music through headphones. That way, she'd be completely unaware of anything. She wasn't on call but if she held her cell phone in her hand, she'd feel it vibrate when it rang. She nodded, pleased she'd come up with a good, solid plan to rest and ignore anything to do with Fletch.

'Molly? Hey, wait up.' She turned to see Alexis running down the corridor after her. 'Hey, speedy, couldn't you hear me?' Alexis puffed as she came to stand next to Molly. 'Where you headed in such a hurry?'

'Home.' Molly started walking again and Alexis fell into step beside her.

'Are you excited about assisting with the surgery tomorrow? I'm green with envy. It's such an incredible opportunity, especially as you're a registrar. I was positive he would have chosen one of the consultants to assist him.' Alexis grinned from ear to ear and nudged Molly. 'Perhaps your shared past, whatever it is, is a good thing.'

'You would think that,' Molly muttered, continuing at a brisk pace. 'You've always got to see the bright side of things.'

'I'd be happy to take your place.' Alexis spread her arms wide as they rounded the corridor, then dropped them immediately. 'Oh, my gosh. It's Roger.' She leaned closer to Molly, her tone quiet and excited. 'How many dates have the two of you had now?'

'Four, if you could call them dates. We've always gone out with a bunch of other people.' Molly forced a smile as the man she'd been casually seeing looked up from the notes he was reading and grinned brightly at both of them.

'Well, hello, ladies. Fancy meeting you in such a corridor as this.' He spread one arm wide to indicate their surroundings. He winked at Molly and she remembered why she liked Roger so much. Not only was he handsome in a boyish kind of way but she always had fun when she went out with him. He reminded her of the life she used to lead before she'd embarked upon this final year of study.

Any final year for a registrar was a difficult one and where before she used to go out dancing, organise hospital fundraising parties and generally be the life of the party, she'd had to put all that aside to focus on the intensity of her studies. Clinics, operating, on-call roster, lectures, assignments, examinations, ward rounds—everything—left little time for socialising. Therefore, when Roger had asked her out a few months ago, and she hadn't been rostered on, she'd gratefully accepted. The consultant physician seemed to be friendly with everyone he met and he'd certainly provided her with a bit of relief from her overwhelming schedule.

Roger leaned forward and wiped a finger down the back of her cheek, near her left ear. 'Been playing dress-up again?' He showed her the bit of white make-up she'd obviously missed removing earlier.

'Oh, gosh. That's from clown patrol earlier today.' She instantly raised her hand to her cheek and rubbed. 'Was that there the whole time?' She stared at Alexis in alarm. 'Why didn't you tell me?'

'Because I didn't see it?'

'What's the problem?' Roger looked quizzically from one tired registrar to the other.

'Only that Molly's been chosen to assist the new visiting research fellow in Surgery tomorrow. It'll be the first time anyone here's seen the procedure being performed. Quite exciting.'

'Really? That's fantastic.'

'And I was standing at the front of the lecture theatre with him as he ran through the procedure. Standing there in front of everyone with clown paint still on my face.' She rubbed her cheek again, annoyed that she hadn't showered when she'd gone home. Fletcher! It was all his fault.

'What time is the surgery scheduled for?'

'Two o'clock,' Alexis answered.

'Why?' Molly was confused.

'I'd like to watch.'

'You're a physician.'

'Doesn't mean I'm not interested in new surgical breakthroughs. Plus...' he brushed his fingers across her cheek again but this time it wasn't to remove make-up but more of a caress. '...I get to see my best girl operate.'

'*Your* best girl?' The question came from a deep male voice, directly behind them. Molly and Alexis turned to see Fletcher walking towards them. He immediately held out his hand to Roger. 'Fletcher Thompson. Visiting research fellow.'

'Roger Armistad. Physician.' The two men shook hands and all Molly wanted to do was to high-tail it out of there as fast as possible. Fletcher and Roger stared at each other for a long moment, as though they were sizing each other up. Molly's heart was pounding so wildly against her ribs, she was positive everyone could hear it.

Fletcher looked at Molly. 'Well, "best girl", I need to arrange a time to meet with you to discuss the procedure in more detail.'

Molly bit her lip and nodded. 'Right.'

'An excellent move, choosing a registrar to assist you rather than an already qualified surgeon,' Roger praised. 'And of course, Molly is *very* good.' He waggled his eyebrows up and down in a suggestive manner.

Alexis started to laugh but, at a glare from Molly, covered it over with a cough. Fletcher didn't seem to notice.

'I've read Dr Wilton's file and it was indeed… impressive. Besides, how are registrars supposed to fully grasp the intricacies of the procedure if they're not involved?'

'True. Very true.'

'Plus, this procedure is best performed out in the field, in Third World countries or places where the medical equipment may not be as up to date as a hospital such as this.' Fletcher indicated their surroundings. 'Consultants are already employed, sometimes even too set in their ways. Whereas a senior registrar, such as Dr Wilton, may be interested, once she's fully qualified, to take these new skills and put them to good use overseas where there is a serious lack of medical staff willing to take on such conditions.'

'Good call.' Roger nodded with approval, then checked his watch. 'Looks like I'm going to be late for clinic.' He winked at Molly again and grinned at Alexis before nodding towards Fletcher. 'See you all later.' He started off down the corridor, then turned and walked backwards. 'Drinks. Pub across the road. Seven o'clock onwards. If you're free.'

'Seven o'clock,' Alexis agreed with a thumbs-up before Roger turned and continued around the corner towards Outpatients. She looked at Molly, then Fletcher and back again. 'And uh…I'd better go, too. I've got patients to see in the ward. I'll do your patients, too,' she told Molly. 'Go home.'

'Thanks, Lexi. I will.'

'See you tomorrow, Dr Thompson. Oh, and if you're interested in volunteers for your next demonstration, put my name at the top of the list. I'm happy to work overseas, helping others.' She grinned before walking off in the opposite direction to Roger.

So there they stood. Molly and Fletcher. In the

middle of a hospital corridor. The two of them alone. Staring at each other. An awkwardness seemed to settle over them for a moment before Fletcher spoke.

'She seems nice. That's Dr Borello, right? The other senior registrar in the surgical programme?'

Molly sighed, then started walking towards the stairs. 'Correct.' Annoyingly, Fletcher kept up with her.

'So what about you?'

Molly stopped as she pushed open the door to the stairwell. 'What about me?'

'Having senior registrars assist me not only helps you in your final exams but also gives you the opportunity to hopefully make different choices once you're fully qualified. We need good doctors overseas, helping out.'

Molly nodded. 'Still saving the world, eh?' She headed down the stairs, pleased that in essentials Fletcher was still the man she'd known. He was willing to help both her and Alexis by providing them with first-hand experience. He was also still involved in his overseas programmes, ones he'd organised and put in place many years ago, his compassionate heart knowing no bounds when it came to giving to others.

'Someone's got to do it.'

Molly continued down the stairs and out into the corridor, where she headed towards the entrance to the hospital. She didn't really want to have another discussion with Fletch about his work as it was one of the main reasons why she'd given him up all those years ago. How could she ever have asked him to stay in a normal, suburban environment and be with her when his whole desire had been to help others? Every time she'd missed him, every time she'd wanted him back, she'd felt guilty for being so selfish. Clearly, seeing him now, it had been the right decision.

'Have you thought about what you might do once you've graduated?' He'd followed her outside.

Molly blinked against the late afternoon sunlight before turning to face him. All the tension drained out of her, the frustration, the annoyance, the need to avoid him. She was so tired. 'Look, Fletch. I'm exhausted. I just want to go home and sleep. I don't want to talk about my career. I don't want to rehash the past. I just—want—to sleep.' There was desperation in her tone as well as deflation. Right now, she had nothing more to give. Not to him, not to her patients, not to anyone. He peered into her eyes for a moment before surprising her by cupping her cheek, his touch comforting and compassionate. It was the way he would have touched her all those years ago, wanting what was best for her.

Time seemed to stand still as she could clearly picture them standing at the airport in almost exactly the same pose. She was saying goodbye to him yet again but this time she was finding it more difficult to let him go.

'That's the final call for my flight. I have to go.'

'I don't want you to go,' she'd said, wrapping her arms around him, never wanting to let him go. They'd had an argument the night before, Fletcher telling her he wanted her to move to Sydney with him, that they could settle there, and Molly had been adamant that as she was pregnant, it was important for her to stay close to her family. In the end, they'd decided to let it go and to discuss it at a later date. Fletcher had kissed her, held her close and made slow, sweet love to her. It had always been so perfect between them and it had been at those times, those moments when they'd been completely lost within each other, that she'd known their marriage had to last. She'd had no idea how that was going to happen, not when she'd been saying goodbye to him yet again.

He'd eased back from her touch, brushing his lips across hers once more before tenderly cupping her face, his touch caring and comforting. 'I may be physically away from you, Molly, but you have my heart. Always.' He'd gazed into her eyes for a moment longer before turning and heading down the walkway towards the waiting aeroplane.

She'd always known that the work he'd left her to do had been necessary. He'd been volunteering to help those less fortunate, gaining credits for his acceptance into the surgical rotation programme. Whenever he'd been home with her, they'd often sat on the patio, gazing up at the stars, snuggling together, Molly listening as he'd told her about extracting a patient's tooth that had been decaying so badly, it had been making the elderly man extremely ill. Or the time he'd delivered a baby on the side of the road, the mother only fourteen years old. Or the time he and the medical team had hiked for three days into the jungle in order to reach a secluded tribe and provide necessary medical treatment.

How had she been supposed to compete with that? Her husband had had a calling, one that had been helping a lot of people and yet all she'd wanted was for him to stay with her…and because she had, she'd felt incredibly selfish.

Now, as they stood, staring at each other, his action of touching her cheek simply an old habit, one he'd probably done quite unconsciously, Molly found it difficult to stop herself from leaning into his touch.

With superhuman effort, she fought the urge and took a step back. Fletcher instantly dropped his hand and shoved it into his trouser pocket, as though the limb clearly had a mind of its own. 'I'm sorry. You clearly are quite tired. Go. Sleep. I'll contact you in the morning to go over the finer points of the surgery so you're as prepared as possible.'

'Thank you.' With that, Molly turned away from him and headed down the street, the warmth from his sweet touch still pulsing through her.

* * *

Fletcher watched her go, trying not to be affected by the way her hips gently swayed from side to side as she walked. Her shoulders were a little hunched over, indicating she was too tired to keep her posture in check. It made him want to scoop her into his arms and carry her home, placing her on the bed as an old-fashioned knight might do for the damsel in distress.

He'd done that in the past. Scooped her up and carried her to bed when she'd fallen asleep on the lounge. He'd watched her sleep, stroking her lovely blonde locks, unable to believe he had the right to brush sweet, tender kisses across her lips, waking her gently so they could make love.

As she rounded the corner, disappearing from his sight, he sighed and shook his head. What was wrong with him? Why on earth was he ogling Molly when he had no real right to do so? He wasn't a free man, in more ways than one. He needed to talk to Molly about legal matters, he needed to tell her that he was seeing someone else but, most of all, he needed to stop himself from giving in to old gestures, old habits.

He turned and headed to the ward, wanting to

talk to his one and only patient, Mr Majors, but even work wasn't enough to distract him from thoughts of Molly. She was…incredible. She was more beautiful than she'd been all those years ago, more alluring, more desirable. The attraction Fletcher still felt towards Molly had taken him completely by surprise. He hadn't expected it and yet, as soon as he'd seen her, talked to her, smiled at her, he'd been unable to stop himself from slipping into those old habits. Teasing her, wanting to hug her, touching her cheek…

It didn't seem to matter that she appeared to be dating that physician he'd met, or that he was seriously involved with Eliza. He simply hadn't been able to control his reaction to her and that was indeed a problem, especially as he had to stand on the other side of the theatre table from her tomorrow. Somehow, between now and then, he had to figure out a way to cope with being around her and yet being completely professional.

How was that possible when, deep down in his heart, he realised she was and would for ever be *his* Molly?

Basically, he was in trouble.

* * *

Why had he come to her hospital? Was he intent on recruiting her once she'd graduated? Was that his main purpose? Or was there something else?

Molly tried her best to put Fletcher Thompson from her mind as she quickly had something to eat, changed into her pyjamas and closed the blinds. It might be only half past five in the afternoon but she was exhausted and tomorrow was a big day. Tomorrow she not only had to stand alongside Fletcher in an operating theatre with a gallery of people—including Roger—watching her every move but she also had to concentrate!

'Oh, Fletcher. Why? Why?' she moaned into her pillow before trying to relax her body. It took a good twenty or so minutes for her eyes to stay closed and her mind to clear.

It felt as if only a few minutes had passed before she heard a knock at her door. 'Huh!' She sat up in bed as the knocking sound came again. She glanced at the clock. 'Six-thirty?' Had she only slept an hour? The knocking came again and she quickly pulled a robe around her cartoon PJs and padded quietly to the door. What now?

It wasn't until she opened the door—early-

morning sunlight surrounding her—that she realised she had indeed slept for over twelve hours.
'It's morning?'

'You see, this is the reason why I chose you to
assist me with the surgery,' Fletcher remarked
as he walked past her into the house. 'You're so
smart and always on the ball.'

'What are you doing?' Molly was still a little
sleepy, a little off guard, a little late in stopping
him. She closed the door behind her and followed
him up the hallway towards the kitchen. It was
only when she saw him standing at her kitchen
table, unloading a bag of groceries, that she even
realised he'd been carrying something.

'I'm making us breakfast. Still like your eggs
scrambled?'

'Fletch.' She sighed with impatience as she
rubbed her eyes. 'Why? Why are you here?'

'We need to discuss the surgery. I need to eat.
You need to eat. I thought we could multitask together.' He was still moving around her kitchen,
opening cupboards here and there, looking for
different utensils before pulling out a chair for
her. 'Sit down, magnificent Molly.' His tone was
reflective. Molly tried hard to ignore the warmth

that spread through her at the name, the one he used to whisper in her ear after they'd made love…but back then he'd said *my* magnificent Molly.

'Fletch.' She sighed again but this time it was with regret. Regret that things hadn't ended well between them. She sat in the chair, too flummoxed to protest any further. She was hungry, she did need to know about the surgery and she knew of old that once Fletcher set his mind to something, it was extremely rare that it changed.

'Excellent!' He grinned at her as he started to prepare food, as though nothing had separated them, as though they were still together, as though he wanted nothing more than to spend time with her.

Was that why he was here? At her hospital? Living next door to her? Choosing her for the surgery? Was Fletcher interested in starting things up again? Was that even possible? The thought made Molly tremble with excited anticipation… as well as dread.

CHAPTER THREE

SURPRISINGLY, IT DIDN'T feel uncomfortable watching Fletcher make her breakfast. He started talking about the surgery, about how he'd discovered the need for the new device, about the earlier prototypes and how, through various tweaks, he'd ended up with the patented product now available to all surgeons worldwide.

'Especially to those doctors working in Third World countries and other places where it's difficult to get to a hospital.'

'Such as Tarparnii,' Molly said after swallowing her mouthful of the most delicious scrambled eggs she'd had in a long time.

'Yes.' He seemed surprised at this. 'Have you been?'

'Just for ten days, not as part of the Pacific Medical Aid team.'

'You went there for a holiday?' Fletcher's eyebrows hit his hairline.

'Cora and her husband adopted a little boy from Tarparnii.'

'Really? Cora's married?'

Molly smiled. 'Stacey, too.'

'Wow. Things have certainly been happening in the Wilton household.'

'Stacey and her husband, Pierce, live in Newcastle with our three younger siblings.'

'You have *three* younger siblings? I remember holding Jasmine. Your stepmother had more children?'

At the mention of Letisha, Molly nodded, a sad smile on her face. 'She did. Jasmine is now almost seventeen.'

'What? No. It can't have been that long.'

Molly chuckled as she finished off her breakfast then sat back, feeling very full but happy. She *was* happy to be chatting with Fletcher again. They'd always connected, right from the very beginning. Even though he'd been dating her friend, Amanda, it had been *she* and Fletch who had chatted on the long, twenty-five-hour plane journey from Australia to England. They'd had the same sense of humour, liked the same music, read the same books. Plus, because Fletch had just finished medical school and Molly had just been accepted, he'd fuelled the fire, telling her how wonderful it was to really be able to help others in a practical way.

Even back then, he'd had plans to change the world, to reach out and help those less fortunate, to provide first-rate medical care to anyone who needed it, regardless of race, gender or financial status. She'd been enamoured with him and then, when he and Amanda had split up, Amanda refusing to go on the tour of Europe and the States, Fletch and Molly had stuck together, becoming friends throughout the tour. By the end of their time together, they'd become…much more than just friends.

'So what are the names of your other siblings?' Fletcher's words brought her thoughts back to the present and she realised he was now beginning to clear the table. She quickly stood up.

'Don't do that. You cooked. The least I can do is clean up.'

'Sit.' He pointed to the chair before reaching for her plate. 'Breakfast comes with full service— and a smile!' He grinned widely at her, his eyebrows raised, his eyes open. The silly face made

Molly laugh and she sat back down, deciding not to argue with him. Perhaps there was the possibility that they could maintain an easy friendship during his stay. 'Tell me about your siblings.'

'OK. Well, there's Lydia, who's just turned ten, and then poor, poor George who is twelve years old and, until Stacey married Pierce, had to put up with being the only boy in a house full of girls. When Cora brought her new son, Ty, home to Australia, George was so delighted to be inheriting yet another male and one that was younger than him, that he seemed to instantly mature.' Molly's sigh was more melancholy than sad. 'Sometimes he reminds me so much of my father.'

Fletcher switched the kettle on to boil to make them both a cup of tea. 'Isn't that a good thing? Your dad's so supportive, so wise.'

Molly lifted her gaze to meet his, staring into his face for a moment before sighing sadly. 'Oh, you don't know.' She closed her eyes for a moment before looking at him once again. 'Of course you don't know. How could you possibly know?'

'Know what?' There was a hint of dreaded anticipation in his question, as though he instinctively knew she was going to deliver bad news.

'My father and Letisha…they both passed away in an accident about six months before we turned thirty. Almost five years ago now.' She shook her head. Her eyes were filled with sadness and there was pain in her tone. 'I can't believe it's been that long already.'

Fletch pulled his chair closer to hers and sat down, taking her hand in his. 'Oh, Molly. I'm so terribly sorry.' He paused for a moment, then shook his head sadly. 'Really I am. I loved them both. You must know that.'

'I do.' She gave him a sad smile. 'They were both so easy to love.'

'You poor thing. You've certainly had your fair share of grief.'

Molly nodded, accepting his compassion but at the same time finding it increasingly difficult not to be affected by his fresh, spicy scent or the way she was unable to stop staring at his mouth as he spoke. She didn't want to think about the way he made her feel, nor the memories he might resurrect if they started down the path of talking about grief. It was too much, especially with the surgery they'd be performing this afternoon. She made sure the lid was firmly on the box of pain she'd hidden away years ago and forced herself to break the contact.

'Wh...er...what about you?' She cleared her throat and folded her arms across her chest. 'Uh...your parents?'

'My parents?' When he spoke, there was a huskiness to his tone. He quickly cleared his throat, as though he, too, didn't want to go down that path, either. 'They still live in Spain. We're still estranged.'

Molly was mildly aware of computing his answer because all she could focus on was the chemistry that existed between them. How was it possible when they hadn't seen each other for such a long time for the tension and attraction still to be as powerful and as prominent as ever? More importantly, how was she supposed to stand opposite him in the operating theatre with a gallery full of spectators and be expected to concentrate rather than staring into his gorgeous eyes?

'I've always liked your eyes.' The whispered words left her lips before she could stop them. She gasped and covered her mouth with her hand.

'Sorry,' she mumbled and stood, needing to put distance between them.

'And I've always liked your—'

'Stop! Don't say it. Don't say anything else.' She stood on the opposite side of the room, ignoring the way her body seemed to instantly ignite with a burning desire, the type of desire she'd only ever felt with Fletcher.

'You're right.' He nodded, then raked a hand through his hair. 'Actually, there is something I need to tell you.' It was only fair she knew about Eliza.

'No!' Molly held up both her hands. 'I can't take any more, at the moment. I don't want to rehash the past; I don't want to talk about other important issues unless they have something to do with the surgery. I have enough to concentrate on for the moment, especially as there will be a gallery of specialists, registrars, interns and a whole plethora of other staff members, watching me perform surgery on Mr Majors with a device I've never used before.'

Fletcher nodded. 'You're right. You're absolutely right. The talks we need to have can wait a while longer.' He crossed his arms. 'I guess it's difficult not to fall back into old habits.'

'Try. We're both very different people from who we were back then.'

'And there are a lot of regrets and hurts still between us.' He nodded again. 'I get the message.'

'Good.' Molly sighed with relief but wasn't sure what to do now. She pointed to the kitchen table. 'Shall we continue with the lesson…for the surgical procedure?' she added quickly.

'Yes.' He turned on his computer tablet so he could continue with the instructions. 'If you look at this diagram, this is the way to ensure the device is in the correct position.'

Molly stared at it, refocusing her mind so she could absorb the information. Not only would she be assisting Fletch during the surgery, but she would be taking over at the crucial moment. It was imperative she get it one hundred per cent correct. She asked him questions and pictured herself actually doing what needed to be done.

'Is it serious?' he asked a while later, his words soft.

She glanced up at him. 'What?'

'You and the physician.'

'Fletch—' She clenched her jaw and glared at him.

'I know. It's none of my business but I guess… I want to know that you're happy.'

'I'm not your concern any more, just like you're not mine.'

'But are you happy?'

'Are you?' she countered and was surprised when he looked away. She frowned. It was clear there was something going on. Fletch coming to Sydney, to her hospital, to her department—it was far too coincidental. She couldn't stop the questions from bubbling over. 'Why *are* you here, Fletcher? Why did you add Sydney General hospital to the end of your tour schedule? Does it have anything to do with me?'

He eased back in his chair and pushed his hands through his hair, sighing heavily. 'The tour was already over-extended and we wanted to concentrate on going to a lot of rural and outback hospitals first, the larger hospitals second.'

'We?'

'Eliza. She's my…er…tour manager, amongst other things.' He mumbled the last bit.

'Where is she?'

'In Melbourne. Her father was diagnosed with kidney cancer. He's just had major surgery to remove the kidney and now he's starting chemotherapy. She's gone home to be with him.' Fletch stopped and sat forward again. 'But to answer your last question, yes. My being here does have something to do with you.'

She watched the way he avoided making eye contact with her as he spoke of his tour manager. Clearly, after working together throughout the duration of the tour, they'd become quite close...but how close? Were they involved? At the thought, a pang of jealousy pulsed through her but she quickly shook it from her mind. She and Fletcher were nothing to each other.

'It's also why I asked Eliza to add Sydney General to the end of the tour schedule.'

'Why?' No sooner was the word out of her mouth than her phone rang. She closed her eyes for a second, the intense bubble she and Fletcher had been inhabiting broken by her crazy ringtone. 'That's Alexis's customised ringtone. I need to answer it.'

'Of course.'

'Lexi?' she said into the phone after connecting the call.

'Mr Majors, your patient for today's surgical procedure, is starting to get nervous and his blood pressure has actually increased. I thought if you could come and talk to him once more about the procedure, he'd calm down. I can call the anaesthetist now to come and review him if that's what you'd prefer.'

'OK. Thanks for letting me know. We'll come in. Give me fifteen minutes.'

'We?' There was intrigue in her friend's tone.

'Fifteen minutes, Lexi. Bye.' Molly disconnected the call, silently berating herself for the slip of tongue, before relating the information to Fletcher.

'Good. Well, Dr Wilton,' he said as he stood. 'I think you're as ready as you can be regarding this afternoon's surgical procedure. Remember to ask me questions and I'll talk you through whatever you need.'

'Thanks.' They both stood there, staring at each other again. She swallowed, trying to ignore the tension and the unspoken questions that seemed to be floating around them. 'Uh…I'd better go shower and get ready.'

'Yes. Good.' He shifted awkwardly, pushing in his chair. 'I'll let myself out.'

'OK.' She edged towards the door, smiling politely as though they really were only colleagues. 'Thanks again for your patience in explaining things.'

'I'm a very patient man.'

Molly closed her eyes at this and shook her head. She clenched her jaw shut to stop herself from saying anything that would open the can of worms she'd just managed to shove the lid on. She looked at him once more before sighing and walking from the room.

Why did he scramble her thoughts as easily as he scrambled eggs? How was it possible that, after all these years, there was still an underlying attraction pulsing between them? They'd both moved on with their lives. She was seeing Roger and, although in her own mind it was nothing serious, until she and Roger had discussed more about the parameters of their relationship she shouldn't be ogling other men, especially not her ex-husband.

She could remember all too clearly the pain and hurt she'd felt the last time they'd said goodbye. Even though they'd both changed, it would be ludicrous to even consider opening herself up to such loss and heartache again.

'It's just not worth it,' she told her reflection as she dried her hair, knowing she needed to get her curls under control so they'd be able to fit into her theatre cap. 'It's over between the two of you. *Very* over.' She switched off the hairdryer and stared at herself in the mirror. 'You're a professional. You can do this. You can stand opposite him in Theatre and you can perform your duties with exceptional flair and expertise.'

With that, she nodded once and finished dressing, wanting to quickly stack the dishwasher before she left, but when she entered the kitchen, she stopped. The place was immaculate, the dishwasher humming quietly as it went through the cycle.

Molly shook her head in bemusement. Although Fletcher might drive her completely to distraction, send her body into a frenzy of tingles and excite her mind with his cleverness, he was also clearly very domesticated. Had he

been like that before? She could well remember
spending time doing the cooking and tidying
with him, the two of them having fun, but in
those days, those early carefree days, it hadn't
mattered what they were doing so long as they
could do it together.

She closed her eyes for a moment, allowing the
good times to wash over her. Sure, in the beginning, she'd felt sort of guilty being so attracted to
him, especially as he and Amanda had broken up,
but, as Fletch had rationalised, he and Amanda
had been growing apart for quite some time.

'This impromptu holiday was our last effort to
see if we wanted to be together,' Fletch had told
her two days after they'd arrived in London. 'We
didn't even last the plane ride over here.' He'd
been sad but not upset. Amanda had already confessed to Molly before they'd left that she hadn't
been sure about Fletcher.

'He's living on the other side of Australia,'
Amanda had said. 'That makes it difficult and
besides, there's this guy at my new job…Bobby.'

'I thought you said he already had a girlfriend.'

'So? I have a boyfriend but—' Amanda had

sighed. 'Bobby is just so…attentive and thought-ful and we definitely click, if you know what I mean.'

'And Fletcher?'

'Fletcher is a genius. He's determined to save the world. How can a woman not be attracted to a man who has such incredible goals? But those goals mean that he tends to spend less time with me and more time saving the world.'

'That's a huge career goal.'

'And he'll achieve it. He has determination in spades.'

'Are you sure you want to come on this trip?' Molly hadn't been able to stop the concern from creeping into her voice. 'I feel as though I'm pres-suring you.'

Amanda had snorted. 'It's not your fault that your sisters can't go with you on your trip. I was devastated to learn that Cora was in hospital and wouldn't be able to go.'

'I'm not sure *I* want to go, especially without them.' Molly had frowned sadly.

'But as Cora said, you need to go—so they can share in your experiences.'

'I wish Stacey would come, too, but then that

would feel even more wrong, the two of us without Cora, but the agreement is that Stacey stays with Cora and I go and have new and exciting adventures, which I will be sharing with them the entire way.'

'Your phone bill's going to be astronomical.' Amanda had put her hand over Molly's. 'I'm glad I'm able to take over one of the pre-paid tickets and Fletcher said he was ready for three weeks of fun overseas to celebrate finishing his medical degree. We're helping you out by taking those two tickets off your hands and you're helping us out by giving us the opportunity to see whether this thing between us is worth pursuing.'

'I hope it is. He does sound like an incredible man but I also don't want to be a third wheel.'

Amanda had shaken her head. 'I don't think that's going to happen. Fletch is a very inclusive sort of guy and, besides, you've just been accepted to medical school—'

'Don't remind me. I'm still not one hundred per cent sure it's what I want,' Molly had interrupted.

'And Fletch has just finished medical school so the two of you will have lots in common.'

And they had…far more than any of them had realised.

Molly opened her eyes, giving herself a mental shake and clearing her thoughts. She shouldn't be taking a trip down memory lane, not when Mr Majors needed to see her. Grabbing her jacket, she pulled it on and reached for her bag and hospital key card before heading out of the front door.

'Ah. Excellent timing,' Fletcher remarked as he closed his door and wound a light red scarf around his neck. 'Shall we walk together?'

'Uh…' It seemed ridiculous to refuse, especially as they were both going to the exact same location. 'Sure.' Molly put her bag onto her shoulder but the strap twisted. Within an instant, Fletch was there, offering assistance, untwisting the strap.

'There you go.'

'Thank you,' she said softly before starting down the path. 'And thank you for cleaning up the kitchen.'

''Twas but the work of a moment.' He waved a hand in the air with a flourish and she couldn't help the smile that instantly sprang to her lips.

'You're still a nutter.'

He shrugged a shoulder as though to say he didn't really mind being thought a nutter. 'So long as I get the laugh.'

'Are you like this in Theatre? Am I going to be standing across the table from a clown?'

He smiled at her. 'Oh, no. In Theatre I am all seriousness. No jokes.'

'I'm sure Mr Majors will appreciate that as well as me.'

They turned the corner, the hospital looming up ahead in the distance. The Sydney spring morning was brisk but not cold, the sun already starting to warm them up. 'We shall be one hundred per cent professional,' he stated, his stride becoming more determined, his tone firm and direct.

'Focusing on the surgery, on Mr Majors' needs, is paramount this morning. The rest can wait.'

And that was the way he remained throughout the day. When they arrived in the male surgical ward, they found Mr Majors propped up on pillows, grinning widely at them both. Fletcher once more explained the procedure to him, answering every question their patient had.

'So my innards are going to be on show to everyone?' Mr Majors asked, an excited gleam in his eyes.

Fletcher nodded. 'Yes, sir.'

'And it will be videoed?'

'It will be recorded, yes.'

'Can I have a copy?'

Molly and Fletcher both raised their eyebrows at this request, looking at each other for a split second before returning their attention to their patient. 'Of course,' Fletcher agreed.

'Excellent.' Pleased this was now sorted out, Mr Majors was more than happy to undergo his pre-anaesthetic review while Fletcher and Molly said goodbye to him. They completed a ward round, Fletcher accompanying Molly and Alexis as they spoke to their other patients and discussed some more interesting cases with the other surgical consultants. Fletcher was often asked for his opinion with everyone listening intently to his answers.

'He's already liked by absolutely everyone,' Alexis told her as she grabbed some lunch. 'Are you sure you don't want to eat anything?'

'Far too nervous.' Molly sipped her coffee. 'This will get me through.'

'Not worried your stomach will growl halfway through the procedure?'

'Well, now I am. Thanks.'

Alexis giggled and the sound helped Molly to relax a little more. 'So…this morning when I called…you said "we". What did that mean?'

Molly looked down at her cup before exhaling slowly. 'It means—and I don't want you to read anything into this because it's really nothing—but Fletcher is staying in the duplex next to mine.'

'What? Really?' Alexis laughed again. 'Isn't that…cosy?'

'No. It's not. He's just my neighbour for a few weeks.' And Molly was positive she could survive that long. It didn't matter that Fletcher was clearly up to something else, that he'd come to Sydney just to see her. Whatever it was, she would deal with it, say goodbye to Fletcher once more and get back to her life. 'Just a few weeks.' She nodded as though glad to get a bit more control over her thoughts. 'Nothing more.'

Alexis raised a querying eyebrow. 'Are you sure about that?'

Molly closed her eyes and whimpered. 'No.'

CHAPTER FOUR

IT WASN'T LONG before it was time for Molly to head to Theatres. Fletcher was just about to enter the male changing rooms as she headed towards the female rooms.

'Hey there. Nervous?' he asked.

She thought about this for a second, then shook her head. 'Not really. More…excited than anything else.'

'Good.' He was still Dr Brisk and Efficient and she had to admit that she liked this version of him. She felt more comfortable around the brilliant Dr Fletcher Thompson, rather than cheeky, adorable Fletch who had made her breakfast this morning. He entered the code for the male changing rooms and, after a brief nod in her direction, disappeared from view.

Molly followed suit, entering the female changing rooms, eager for this unique opportunity to begin. At the moment, she felt pure gratitude towards Fletch for allowing her to assist him in Theatre. The fact that he was going to ensure Alexis also had the opportunity to assist him at a later date indicated the level of understanding and decency in the man. Years ago, Amanda had described him as a genius, a man who was going to 'save the world', and all these years later Molly was pleased to see that he hadn't wavered from that initial goal.

Mr Majors arrived in the theatre anteroom a moment later and both Molly and Fletcher were more than happy to begin the process. They spoke to their patient, who was nicely drowsy from his pre-med, and after reassuring him once more they wheeled him into the waiting theatre.

Molly joined Fletch at the scrub sink, their backs to the upstairs gallery where many of her colleagues had gathered in order to watch and take as many notes as they could.

'Are you going to look up at the gallery?' Fletcher asked as he used the nail brush to scrub his hands.

'No. As far as I'm concerned, they're not there.'

'So when I'm talking and giving instruction, it's as though I'm talking directly to you?'

'And the rest of the staff in the theatre, yes.'

'OK. I want this to be a good experience for you, Molly. Something to help you in your final oral examination when you need to discuss new invasive procedures and techniques. You're an excellent doctor, from what I've seen. You deserve to pass with flying colours.'

'Thank you, Fletch.' Molly looked up at him, not only hearing the sincerity of his words but seeing it in his eyes. Fletcher believed in her. His words had once more filled her with courage that she could follow his lead and assist him with this surgery without making a fool of herself.

The theatre sister joined them at the scrub sink, asking Fletcher a question about the surgery. He answered it succinctly, Molly listening closely, remembering when he'd told her the same thing over their impromptu working breakfast.

When they'd finished scrubbing and were gowned and gloved, Molly took her place on the opposite side of the table, glad she had her back to the gallery of people above.

'Are the microphones and cameras on?' Fletcher asked as he looked up into the gallery. A few people were cupping their ears, indicating the sound wasn't on. Molly was glad of this because she would have been mortified if her personal conversation with the lead surgeon at the scrub sink had been broadcast to the entire gallery!

A loud squeal came through the system before the scout nurse readjusted the volume switch.

'Can everyone hear me now? Are the monitors working? Someone give me a thumbs up,' he said. Molly was impressed with how relaxed he was but, then again, he'd been travelling around doing exactly this—giving lectures and performing the surgery so others like herself could learn. He really was quite remarkable.

When her gaze met his across the operating table, she couldn't hide the admiration in her eyes. Fletcher's eyes widened perceptibly, as though he was clearly aware of exactly what she was thinking. He raised one eyebrow, or at least she thought he had. It was difficult to tell beneath his protective eye wear, theatre cap and mask.

'Let's begin.' He continued to stare into her eyes for a fraction of a second longer and when Molly gave him a brief nod, he began his monologue of instructions.

His invention really was quite ingenious. A

ready-made stent, which could be applied to various parts of the body. Once inserted correctly, the spring-loaded mechanism was deployed and the device would then open, holding firmly in place. Even in a large hospital, such as this one, the surgery he was performing would have taken close to two hours but with his device the surgery time had been cut in half.

'Even if you're in the middle of a jungle, once you understand the particulars of the procedure—' He stopped talking to the gallery for a moment and asked Molly to reposition the retractor a little more to the left. 'It's quite straightforward. And to prove it, Dr Wilton will be the one to do the honours and insert the device.'

Molly wasn't surprised at this. It was the main thing they'd discussed at breakfast, and as she shifted so Fletcher could take the retractor from her she picked up the device, which was like a very short clamp with the stent attached to the end. With care and precision, she inserted it, just the way Fletcher had described to her.

Although she was aware of the cameras in the room, no doubt providing the viewers in the gallery with a close-up of her hands, she didn't waver or shake, but once the stent was in position she breathed an audible sigh of relief. Fletcher chuckled beneath his mask and when she briefly met his gaze, she could see pride in his eyes. He was proud of her and again that made her feel so wonderful. A warmth spread through her, a warmth of awareness at how lovely it was to be appreciated. Still she wasn't at all sure how he could affirm her and make her feel incredibly feminine with just one look.

'Well done, Dr Wilton. I'd give you a clap but that's hardly appropriate at the moment,' he joked and received a smattering of laughter from the rest of the theatre team. No doubt the people in the gallery were chuckling as well and once more she was highly aware of how suited he was to this work. He was natural, charming and informative. Not to mention brilliant, handsome and even sexier than she remembered.

Molly snapped her thoughts back into place because even though the stent was now correctly in place, there was still more to be done to ensure Mr Majors would make a full and uncomplicated recovery. Thankfully, the rest of the surgical procedure continued without a hitch and soon she was pulling off her gloves and mask as Mr Majors was wheeled away to Recovery.

The gallery was emptying out as people returned to their busy schedules and as Fletcher came to stand beside her at the bins, de-gowning alongside her, she was unable to wipe the enormous grin from her face.

'Wow. I haven't seen that smile in a very long time.'

'I'm just so relieved the surgery is over and that I didn't stuff up.'

'You wouldn't have stuffed up, Molly. Not only are you a gifted surgeon but you apply yourself to instruction. All that studying we did bright and early this morning was well worth it, don't you think?' He put his arm around her shoulders and gave her a little squeeze.

She didn't pull away from him, didn't want to. It was nice to feel his arm there, to be close to him, to be able to breathe in that glorious scent of him, even after he'd been standing at the operating table for the past hour. Molly glanced up at him.

'And silly me suspected you of having ulterior motives when you turned up for breakfast...'

She trailed off, remembering those intense and slightly awkward moments. Her gaze lowered and she stared at his mouth for a second, a thousand different memories flooding her mind, memories of all those other times when Fletch had had every right to press his lips to hers. She tried not to sigh at the memory of those incredible, powerful kisses they'd shared. Ever since the first time he'd kissed her, the chemistry between them had been strong, frightening and very natural... as though it was meant to be.

Fletcher cleared his throat, his arm around her shoulder starting to feel more of a draw-you-closer hug rather than a simple congratulations-well-done hug. Molly's heart rate had increased without her realising it and when she finally raised her gaze back to meet his, it was to find him looking down at her with the same repressed desire she'd seen in his eyes years ago.

Where she'd thought nothing could remove the smile of elation from her face, the thought of Fletcher dipping his head and claiming her lips with his own was enough to momentarily make her forget her earlier triumph.

'Molly.' The way he spoke her name was filled

with confusion and repressed desire. It was as though he, too, was trying to fight the attraction that was so natural between them.

'Congratulating Dr Wilton on a job well done?' Sister asked, and it was only then that Molly remembered that Fletch still had his arm around her. She instantly stepped away, her earlier elation now starting to wane.

'Excuse me. I need to change out of my scrubs. I still have clinic to get through.' With that, she headed off before he could say anything else. Thankfully, Sister asked him another question about the surgical procedure, detaining him long enough for her to get away. The last thing Molly needed was to have Fletch follow her to the changing rooms and continue their staring contest. She also hadn't wanted to hang around and be the subject of Theatre Sister's questions. The less the staff at Sydney General knew about her prior relationship with Fletcher Thompson, the better.

'What was that all about?' Alexis burst into the female changing rooms just as Molly had finished showering and dressing in the clothes she'd worn to the hospital that morning.

'What? The operation?' Molly grinned at Alexis before picking up a brush.

'Who cares about the operation?' Alexis spread her arms wide. 'I'm talking about Fetching Fletcher.'

'Fetching Fletcher?' Molly raised her eyebrows at the name, a slight smile twitching at her lips.

Alexis shrugged and dropped her hands. 'It's what most of the females around the hospital are calling him.'

Molly looked at her reflection, imagining the hoot of laughter and immense preening Fletch would undertake if she told him about the nickname. She closed her eyes for a split second, then shook her head, annoyed that she knew him so well, could predict his response.

'But stop trying to change the subject.' Alexis pointed a finger at her.

Molly finished tying her hair back and put her brush into her locker. 'What *is* the subject?'

'You and Fletcher. How long has that been going on?'

Molly instantly looked away. She liked Alexis. The two of them were good friends and, as such, she didn't know if she could blatantly lie to her. 'Uh…why do you ask?'

'Uh…because the microphones were still on in the theatre while the two of you had your little tête-à-tête.'

'What?' Molly glared at her friend in shock. 'You…heard us…*that* was being broadcast into the gallery? Who else was there? Were there more people there?' Molly dropped down onto the bench seat near the lockers and covered her face with her hands. 'Oh, no. No, no, no.'

'It's OK. It's OK.' Alexis sat down beside her. 'By the time you two started talking, everyone had filed out. As clinic is starting later today, I thought I'd wait around for you. So…come on.' Alexis's excitement wasn't waning one little bit. Molly looked at her with dismay. 'How do you know him? Did you used to date? You must have with the way he was all right up against you.' She draped her arm around Molly's shoulders and brought her face close. 'Close enough to kiss you.'

Molly closed her eyes as she delivered the answer to Alexis's questions. 'Yes, I know Fletcher. Very well. And yes, we used to…sort of date…

in that…' she opened her eyes and looked at her friend '…I used to be married to him.'

'What?' It was Alexis's turn to explode and she jumped up from the seat, staring at Molly as though she'd just grown an extra head. 'You were married? To *him*?'

'Yes.'

'Molly, I don't know if you've noticed but the man is gorgeous. Why aren't you still married to him?'

'I was young, Alexis. Very young.'

'When? When was all this marriage thing?'

'I was eighteen and I met him on an overseas tour and…we hit it off straight away and then… a few weeks later…well, we were in Las Vegas and…uh…one thing led to another and…' She shrugged her shoulders.

'You got married in Vegas!'

'I know. Totally cliché, right?'

'But how? Why did it end?'

Molly sighed heavily. 'Just because he's gorgeous, doesn't mean he's the easiest person in the world to live with.'

Alexis gasped, and Molly quickly continued, lest her friend should get the wrong idea. 'Not that he was ever abusive or anything like that. No, no, no.' Alexis sighed with relief at this news. 'Just that there are many reasons why marriages break down. Ours lasted two years and ended with both of us agreeing that we'd jumped into things far too quickly.'

'Hold on.' Alexis held up her hands for a moment. 'You married him when you were eighteen? That's like…sixteen years ago.'

'Correct.'

'And when was the last time you saw him… er…before he came here?'

'A few months before my sisters and I turned twenty-one.'

'So it's been a good fourteen years since you last saw him and he's not married anyone else? Not been engaged even?'

Molly shrugged her shoulders. 'I don't know. I'm presuming there's someone. I mean, look at him. Why wouldn't there be a woman in the wings?' She thought about the way he'd talked about his tour manager, wondering again if he was involved with the woman. Then again, if he was involved with the woman, why would he have been…looking at her the way he had been after surgery?

'And how did you feel about the way he was gazing longingly into your eyes?' Alexis leaned closer again. 'And what about Rah-rah Roger?'

'What about him? There's nothing between Fletcher and I. Nothing except history.' Molly massaged her temples with her fingers. 'And Roger is just…Roger.'

'*Just* Roger?'

'You know that's not what I meant. He's a nice guy. He helps me to loosen up, to release the stress.'

'Oh, really?' Alexis waggled her eyebrows up and down suggestively.

'It's not like that. We're not serious, we're just having fun.'

'Fun?' Alexis's smile increased.

Molly rolled her eyes and shook her head. 'The real thing I need to be focused on right now is what to do about the digital recording of Mr Majors' operation.'

'Just tell Fetching Fletcher what happened and ask him to ensure the end of the recording is properly edited.' Alexis shrugged her shoulders as though the solution was that simple.

'That makes perfect sense. I'll talk to Fletch.'

'He strikes me to be a very reasonable man.'

Molly closed her eyes for a moment, speaking softly. 'A man who has a devastating effect on my equilibrium.'

Alexis clapped her hands with excitement, clearly delighted with this news. 'You still love him.'

'I will always love Fletcher,' Molly agreed, looking at her friend. 'But I'm not *in love* with him.' She looked pointedly at the clock on the wall. 'If we don't get a wriggle on, we'll be even later for clinic.' The two of them left Theatres and headed to the outpatient clinics.

'We're going to be out of here rather late this evening,' Alexis murmured as they collected their patient lists and headed towards their respective consulting-room doors.

'Never a truer word was spoken, Dr Borello.' Fletcher's deep voice rang out through the clinic corridor, a patient list in his hands.

'You're helping with the clinic?' Alexis was

the first to speak as she and Molly just stared at him for a moment.

'I heard you were short staffed.' He looked at Molly, as though trying to gauge her reaction. 'Thought I'd lend a hand.'

Molly nodded and smiled politely. 'Thank you, Fletcher. Much appreciated. Uh…' She hesitated for a second, knowing she needed to talk to him but unsure how to begin. 'Can I speak to you for a moment?' she asked, trying to block Alexis's big grinning face from her peripheral vision. She motioned to her consulting room and within another breath she was closing the door behind him, the two of them once again in close quarters.

'Something wrong?' Fletch asked when Molly paced back and forth behind the desk.

'Yes. As a matter of fact there is.' She stopped and looked at him, then came right out and told him about what Alexis had heard in the gallery.

'Ah. So we need to ensure the file is edited correctly. Right. I'll take care of that.'

'Oh. Thank you.' Molly sighed with relief, her earlier smile starting to return. 'Thank you for this morning, for the coaching, for the opportunity to assist. It really has been a dream come true.'

'You did an excellent job.'

'Only because you were an excellent teacher.'

'Do you know, out of all the times I've instructed this surgical procedure, I'd have to say today's was my favourite.'

'Really?'

'Yes. Once I'm done here, at the end of next week to be precise, my fellowship is officially over so it was nice to have that "everything going according to plan" theatre experience before it ended.'

'What will you do next? Head back overseas?'

He shook his head. 'I have two months to write up my final findings of the fellowship.'

'Where will you go to do that?'

He shrugged. 'Melbourne, perhaps. Or Brisbane or even here in Sydney.'

'Don't stay in Sydney,' she quickly replied, for the last thing she wanted was for Fletch to continue hanging around her hospital. 'Too much… er…pollution.'

He smiled at that, as though he knew exactly what she was trying to do. 'You don't want me living close to you? Next door, for example?' There was a teasing to his tone.

'No. No offence but…no.'

'None taken. You're right, our lives are on different paths now but—' The light went from his eyes and his lips drew into a straight line. She knew that look. Something was wrong and he wasn't doing a very good job of hiding it. He raked a hand through his hair, then fidgeted by brushing imaginary strands of thread from his suit. He seemed to be weighing things up, deciding whether or not to tell her whatever it was he had to say. The longer he lingered, the more concerned she became.

'Fletcher, what is it?' There was a hint of veiled panic in her words. She controlled it as best she could. 'Are you sick? Do you need my help?'

'No. No. I'm well, but I do have something to tell you. I was going to wait until later but I don't know when later is.'

'You're talking in riddles.'

'I know.' He exhaled harshly. 'I'm just trying to figure out the right way to deliver the news.'

'Oh, just blurt it out. Rip the sticking plaster

off and get it done with. You know how I don't like suspense.'

'True. OK. Here goes.' He rubbed his hands together, then pointed to the chair, pulling it out a little. 'Perhaps you should sit down.'

'I'm fine so just tell me what's wrong.' The words were spoken between gritted teeth.

'I've come to see you about a divorce.'

'Why? We're already divorced. Why would you need to see me?''

'Well…because we're not.'

'Not?' Her frown was deep. 'What are you talking about? We got divorced.'

'Actually…' He slowly shook his head. 'We didn't.'

Molly opened and closed her mouth several times as she continued to stare at him in disbelief. 'We…we…we what now?'

'We're still married. Molly, you're still my wife.'

CHAPTER FIVE

MOLLY SLUMPED DOWN into the chair and stared straight ahead, clearly trying to compute what he was saying. 'We're still…?' She shook her head. 'How is that…?'

She was clearly speechless, which was not usual for her and made him a little worried as to what she might do or say next. He tried to smooth things over a bit more. 'I know this is a bit of a shock.'

'A bit?' She looked at him. 'But I remember signing the divorce papers and sending them back to the lawyer. Then quite a while later, I received a large envelope back from the law firm. That was the divorce decree.'

'You did?' Now it was his turn to frown. 'So you actually have a piece of paper stating that we're officially divorced?'

'Yes.'

'Can I see it?'

Molly nodded. 'Sure. It's in a box somewhere in Stacey's shed in Newcastle.'

'Would she mind digging it out for me?'

'I'll call her when I get home tonight.'

'Thanks.' Fletcher sat down on the edge of the desk, deep in thought, a frown furrowing his brow. 'But you do remember seeing it? Actually reading the piece of paper that stated our divorce was final?'

Molly bit her lip and looked down at her hands. 'Well…not exactly.' She sighed, then reluctantly met his gaze.

'So you didn't see the official paper?' His tone was a little harsh and he saw her flinch a little. 'Sorry. This is—'

'This is doing my head in,' she interrupted, standing from the chair and pacing around the consulting room.

'Did you look at the paper?' he asked again, ensuring his tone wasn't so accusing.

'I didn't.' She spread her arms wide. 'I couldn't do it, OK? I couldn't bring myself to look at the piece of paper that stated I was no longer your wife.'

'What did you do?'

'I put it in a box, along with the other memories I had of you and…and…' she wrung her hands together '…and the rest of our time together. In a box. Taped shut. Never to be opened again.' Molly closed her eyes as though desperate to get her emotions under control.

Seeing her reaction, watching the pain cross her face as she mentioned their past, made him clench his jaw. He'd hurt her. Badly. He'd caused her so much emotional distress with the terrible things he'd said to her. Every time he thought about it, his gut churned with displeasure. There was no way he could go back and change the past and, although he'd apologised to her time and time again, he wasn't sure he could forgive himself for just how much he'd hurt her.

Silence engulfed the room. Repressed memories, harsh words, tears and heartbreak filled the air. 'It was such a difficult time, Fletch.' Her words were soft. 'You know that.'

'Yes. It was.' He stood and placed his hands on her shoulders. Molly opened her eyes and looked at him. 'For both of us.' He gazed down at the woman who had stolen his heart so long ago. How was it possible she was even more beautiful now, when back then he'd thought her to be the most stunning woman he'd ever met? His Molly—and she really was *his* Molly, in deed, at least.

The instant he'd seen her again, dressed as a clown, her face covered in make-up, a crazy wig covering her gorgeous blonde hair, which was somehow much curlier now than it had been back then, every fibre of his being had returned to life, as though he'd finally discovered the answer to the secrets of the universe. Everything else had been forgotten. His work. His plans. The new life he was trying to make for himself. His new life with…Eliza.

Yet when he looked at Molly, it was as though he was making a mistake. Eliza was an amazing, easy-going woman and the two of them got along very well but…she wasn't Molly. It was wrong, of course. Wrong to compare them when they were both such different women.

'Fletch?' Her voice was soft as she continued to gaze up at him. He tried to school his thoughts, tried not to be drawn in by her sparkling eyes or her tempting mouth. He swallowed again but didn't drop his hands.

'Yes?' What was she going to ask him? Could she feel it, too? The heightened awareness, the awakened memories and the overwhelming need to do something about it? This moment was far more intense than the one they'd shared in her kitchen that morning. This time they didn't have a table between them. They were close. Too close. If he angled his head a little lower, he could touch his lips to hers, taste her sweet sensations once more and—

'Why do you think we're still married?'

Her question was like a bucket of iced water, freeing his mind from the allure of reliving the past. Fletch dropped his hands back to his sides and took a big step back, not only needing to put some distance between them but also to remember he was romantically linked to another woman. Where was his brain?

'Because we are.' He walked towards the door, then checked his watch. 'Clinic should have started ten minutes ago.' Fletch straightened his tie before shoving both hands into his trouser pockets. 'Why don't we have dinner tonight and we can go over everything then?'

Molly immediately shook her head and pointed

to herself. 'Hates suspense, remember? Just give me the short version. Didn't you receive a divorce decree from the lawyers as well? I just don't understand—'

'I couldn't look at mine, either,' he interrupted.

'What?'

'When my copy arrived from the lawyers, I couldn't look at it, either. Like you, I didn't want to read the piece of paper that told me you were no longer my wife and so I left it with the rest of my stuff at the storage unit and headed overseas.'

Molly frowned. 'None of this makes any sense, Fletcher. Your uncle was the one organising our divorce. You told me it was all under control, that he would sort everything out.'

'I know but…he was old and almost retired at that stage. Although he owned the law firm his sons were trying to phase him out.' Fletch looked up at the ceiling as though expecting answers to fall from the sky. 'It was a comedy of errors.'

'I'm not laughing.'

'Neither am I.' He stared into her eyes. 'Basically, my uncle was getting forgetful. His sons only gave him the most straightforward cases to do and ours was definitely straightforward.'

'So how on earth did he stuff it up? I signed those papers.'

'I know but it turns out…I missed one of the signature points.'

'What? Then why weren't you notified? Why didn't someone hound you until you signed them? They're your family. Surely they would have been able to track you down overseas?'

'Apparently my uncle tried, several times, but was unsuccessful in getting word to me. And then…'

'What?' Molly spread her arms wide with exasperation. He didn't blame her for feeling that way. He'd felt the same when he'd learned the truth.

'He died.'

'Oh.' She dropped her arms back to her sides and frowned. 'Surely someone took over his cases? Why didn't they—'

'They thought it was all taken care of. When I clarified everything with my cousin earlier this year, he said that sometimes things fall through the cracks. The person who took over my uncle's small workload glanced at the file and thought it was complete. Apparently, my uncle hadn't made clear notes detailing what still needed to be accomplished.' Fletcher tapped the side of his head. 'He kept everything up here.' Just like Fletcher's own father. Stubborn, proud and arrogant. He knew now it had been a complete mistake to allow the family law firm to take care of the divorce but back then he'd been hurting, confused and just wanting it all to be taken from his shoulders. When his uncle had offered, he'd jumped at the chance, his cousins assuring him that it was a no brainer.

'Wait. You've known about this for a while? How long?'

'About four months.'

'Four months! And you're just getting around to telling me now?'

'Molly, I've been travelling and this was hardly something we could discuss over the phone or via email.'

She nodded slowly. 'So you added Sydney General to the end of your tour list just so you could come here in person and deliver the news? Hey, Molly, assist me in Theatre…oh, and by the way, we're still married!'

'That's not what—'

'What, Fletcher?' She stood there with her

hands on her hips, her green eyes blazing with anger. 'That's not what you intended?'

He stared at her, unable to look away from her stunning beauty. Even when she was angry, she was still so incredible, so vibrant. How could he have forgotten about Molly's fiery determination?

'You didn't intend to come here and turn my life upside down and inside out?' she continued when he didn't speak. 'What?' She spread her arms wide and glared at him. 'Say *something*.'

'It's just that…you're so—' He stopped himself. It wasn't fair to tell her how beautiful she was when she was angry. He'd done that in the past, teased her out of her anger, made her smile, held her close, loved her slowly and intimately. Fletcher shook his head. What was it about this woman that made him forget everything? Made him forget why he was here? Why they were having this conversation?

'When I discovered the file—'

'Four months ago!'

'Yes, four months ago, I knew it wasn't something I could just talk to you about over the phone or by letter or—'

'Or get the solicitors to deal with? That's their

job, Fletch. They could have contacted me and told me everything I needed to know. But oh, no.' She whirled around and stalked behind the desk as she ground the words out. 'The great and powerful Fletcher Thompson chooses to grace our hospital with his presence, to teach us—the little people—about his brilliance and then, oh, by the way, Molly, we're still married!'

Molly slammed her hands onto the desk. 'I mean—why? How did you discover the letter? Why didn't you discover it years ago? Why *now*?'

Fletcher glanced at the clock on the wall behind her head and shook his head. 'It's complicated, Molly.'

'Don't you try and use that pacifying tone on me. It doesn't work. Answer me, Fletcher.'

'You're starting to get a little agitated so why don't we discuss this later, when we don't have a waiting room full of patients? How about dinner tonight? We can discuss things in more detail then.'

Molly closed her eyes and massaged her temples and he knew of old that her head was starting to pound. In some ways they knew each other so well and yet in others, it was as though they were complete strangers. She had every right to ask the questions she was asking but he was also aware that her voice had started to rise and the last thing he wanted right now was to draw attention to them. He'd offered to help out in the clinic so that Molly could finish work on time and then he'd planned to invite her to dinner at one of his favourite restaurants in Sydney, where he could calmly explain the situation to her, tell her about Eliza, how he needed her to sign the divorce papers so that he could marry Eliza early next year.

Clearly, none of that had happened and now they were already starting to fall behind with their patient lists.

'I can't do dinner tonight.' Her tone was softer, filled with a level of defeat. That tone only added to his guilt because he knew she was giving in, letting him win for the sake of their patients. 'It's been a big enough day for me so if you don't mind, can we leave it until later?'

'Of course,' he repeated, seeing for himself just how tense she was. He could well remember what it was like during his own final year of surgical training, trying to juggle everything.

At the knock on her consulting-room door, she

jumped as the noise startled her. This was yet another indication of just how tired she was and he wished there were something he could do to make life easier for her. Instead, he was positive that his presence here, at her hospital, was making things worse.

'Yes?' she called, directing her voice towards the door.

Alexis popped her head around. 'Sorry to intrude but the patients are starting to crowd the waiting room.'

'Thanks, Alexis.' Molly nodded firmly. 'Would you mind showing Fletcher to his consulting room, please?'

'Uh…sure.' Alexis raised her eyebrows in question but then looked at Fletcher and smiled. 'This way, Fetching Fletcher. Thanks for saving us from being here for hours on end.'

'Fetching Fletcher?' He grinned at the name as he followed Alexis out of Molly's consulting room. 'Is that my new nickname?' He shut Molly's door behind him but could have sworn he heard her groan with exasperation. Clearly she knew about the name and no doubt thought his ego would inflate even more. The thought made him smile. Ah, Molly. Always wanting to bring his ego down a peg or two.

'Here's your consulting room,' Alexis said and pointed to the paper he'd put into his shirt pocket. 'And I see you have your patient list so you should be all set to go.' She quickly explained the system to him, letting him know how things worked before turning on her heel and heading to her own consulting room. Alexis stopped for a moment and looked at him over her shoulder, fixing him with a serious stare.

'Don't hurt Molly.'

'That's not my intention.'

'And yet I have the distinct feeling you will.'

Fletcher glanced down at the ground for a moment before raising his gaze to meet Alexis's once more. 'I have the feeling you might be right... and I hate that.'

Thankfully, Molly was able to finish with her clinic patients before Fletcher.

'I can't believe how quickly we've managed to get through the patient lists,' Alexis stated as she came into Molly's consulting room as she finished writing up the last set of patient notes.

'I'm sure it's all down to the great and wonderful Fetching Fletcher.'

'And I can't believe you called him that to his face.' Molly glanced up at her friend, a small smile on her lips.

'I call it as I see it.' Alexis shrugged. 'And speaking of speaking—'

'Which we weren't.'

'Well, I was.' Her friend chuckled. 'Did you have a little chat with FF to ensure he has the recording edited without the X-rated version tagged onto the end?'

Molly closed the case notes, then stood, picking up the pile of notes and X-rays so she could return them to the clerk. 'It was hardly X-rated, Lexi.' She walked past her friend, edgy to get out of the clinic without bumping into Fletcher. 'But yes, I did.'

'And?'

'And of course he's going to edit it. It would be unprofessional otherwise.' Molly frowned, thinking back to her conversation with him, the one she'd forced from her mind for the past few hours while she'd been concentrating on her patients. How was it possible she was still married to him?

She handed in the notes and X-rays, thanked the staff and said goodnight. Alexis stopped her at the door. 'Aren't you going to wait for him?' She looked around covertly, as though checking no one could hear their conversation. 'Go out for dinner? Drink some wine? Talk over old times?'

'Alexis, stop!' Molly cut her friend off. 'Whatever happened between Fletcher and myself ended years ago. Our lives have run very different courses and that's all there is to it. Now, if you don't mind, I'm very tired and I still have to check on Mr Majors, go home, write up my notes from the operation while everything is still fresh in my mind and then hopefully get some sleep without being called into the hospital for any patient emergencies.'

'Right. Of course.' Alexis pretended to zip her lip then looked intently at her friend. 'I don't want to see you get hurt.' Her words were filled with sincerity.

'Then why are you throwing me at him? Have dinner! Drink wine!'

Alexis shrugged. 'Playing devil's advocate? I'm just making sure your head hasn't been turned by his good looks and easy-going manner.'

Molly smiled and shook her head. 'It hasn't. Believe me.'

Alexis stared at her for another moment before hugging her. 'I'm on call tonight so I'll do my best not to be needing any extra help in Theatres.' She crossed her fingers, both of them knowing that, no matter what they did, if there was an accident and more staff were required, then there was nothing either of them could do. It was their job.

'Thanks. I'll see you tomorrow,' she said before heading to Intensive Care where Mr Majors was doing a superb job of recovering from his surgery. The entire time she was there, she kept expecting Fletcher to enter the ward.

'Are you waiting for someone?' Sister asked.

'No. Why?' Molly answered a little too quickly.

'You just keep checking the door.' Sister waggled her eyebrows up and down. 'Then again, so do the rest of us. Fetching Fletcher's got to come around at some point to check on his one and only patient, right? We all hoped he'd come with you but—'

Molly tuned out Sister's words, preferring to concentrate on writing up Mr Majors' notes,

STILL MARRIED TO HER EX!

extremely pleased with his progress. 'The med-
ications I've prescribed,' she interjected when
Sister paused for a breath, 'should be enough to
get him through the night but, of course, if there
are any problems or queries, give me a call. Immediately.'

Molly left the ICU, stopping by her locker and
collecting her bag before finally walking out of
the hospital door just before seven o'clock in the
evening.

As it was dark, she debated whether to take
a taxi but it wasn't raining and it really wasn't
that far. She set off at a brisk pace, allowing her
thoughts to start whirling. She needed to call
Stacey, to get her to find that envelope, to check
for herself that what Fletch was saying was the
absolute truth. It wasn't that she didn't believe
Fletch, he certainly had no reason to lie about
this, but more because she didn't believe the
entire situation. How could she have been so
careless back then? Why hadn't she opened the
envelope? Checked exactly what it was the lawyers had been sending her?

But she hadn't been strong enough. To see it
written in black and white that she was no longer

Fletcher's wife, that she no longer had any right to demand his time and attention, had been more than she could bear. She'd already been through so much emotional turmoil with the ba—

'No.' She spoke the word out loud as she continued to stride down the street. There was no point in taking her thoughts anywhere near that topic. Instead she pulled her phone from her pocket and called Stacey.

'I need you to check something for me,' she stated and quickly gave Stacey an update on the situation, that the divorce documents hadn't been signed correctly. 'I need you to find that envelope and check.'

'Do you really think you're still married to Fletcher?' It was clear her sister was incredibly puzzled.

'I don't know, Stace. That's why I need you to find the envelope.' Molly had a difficult time keeping the distress from her tone.

'Of course. Of course,' Stacey returned, instantly placating. 'I'll look for it now. Jaz can read the younger kids bedtime stories tonight.'

'Thanks, Stace.'

'Hey, how did the surgery go?'

'The surgery was fantastic. The patient tolerated the procedure very well and is presently on his way to making a full recovery.'

'And how did it feel having all those people watching you?'

Molly opened the front gate to her place. 'I forgot about them. Fletch gave me clear and concise directions as well as explaining the procedure to those in the gallery.'

'He sounds like quite a good teacher,' Stacey mused out loud. Molly shifted her bag in order to get her house keys out, not wanting to think about just how incredible Fletch really was at teaching, especially as she could remember with perfect clarity some of the more sensual lessons he'd taught her during their short marriage.

'I'm home now,' she told her sister, a briskness to her tone as she shoved those past erotic images away. 'Can you look for that envelope, please?'

'Yes. Yes, of course,' Stacey answered, compassion in her tone. 'I'll call you back when I've found it.'

'I don't care what time it is, just call me as soon as you find it.' Molly put her key into the door and opened it, exhaustion really starting to take hold as she dropped her bag to the floor and headed to the kitchen for a drink.

'Right. Talk soon.' Stacey blew a kiss down the phone before disconnecting the call.

Molly put her phone onto the kitchen table before taking out a small bottle of juice from the fridge. Her energy reserves were so low she didn't even have enough to make herself a warm drink. Taking the juice through to the lounge room, she sank down into the large, comfortable chair and closed her eyes for a moment.

What a day. In fact ever since Fletch had arrived in Sydney, he'd turned her world upside down. It was more difficult to control her thoughts when she was around him, difficult not to close her eyes and remember the happiness they'd once shared whenever she breathed in his gorgeous scent.

Whatever she'd been feeling since his return, however she might have interpreted his behaviour, especially as the attraction between them still seemed to be smouldering beneath the surface, it was clearly nothing more than residual emotion. Their marriage had ended abruptly, filled with pain and regret, and she had no idea how to move past that. Feelings of inadequacy, of failure. For far too long she'd felt as though she'd failed him, not only as a wife but as a mother—

'No. Don't think about it.' Even all these years later, the loss she'd suffered was still such a deep wound, such an anguish she wondered if she'd ever truly recover from it. Instead, she'd focused on her career and her family. That had provided her with enough healing balm to cover over the wound. Molly yawned and shifted in the chair, curling into the cushions, accepting the comfort the inanimate object provided.

The knock at the door startled her. Molly sat up, instantly alert. She looked at her watch, astonished to discover several hours had passed since she'd arrived home. Who could be coming around at this hour?

She headed to the door as the person waiting there knocked once more. When her phone started ringing, she groaned and took a quick detour to the kitchen where she'd left it. It was Stacey.

'Just a minute,' she called to whoever was at the door. 'Stacey?' she said into the phone.

'I've found the envelope.' Stacey's voice was

sombre yet held a hint of uncertainty. 'Are you sure, Molly?'

'Just a second, someone's at the door,' she told her sister, but the instant she opened the door and saw just who was standing there she spoke to her sister again, her gaze not breaking from the man before her. Why was it that at the first sight of Fletch, who was dressed comfortably in jeans and light jumper, her heart had started beating out an erratic rhythm?

'Fletcher's at the door. I'm putting you on speaker. Go ahead, Stacey. Open the envelope.'

At her words, Fletcher raised his eyebrows. They stood there, on either side of the threshold, communicating with no need for words. He knew exactly what was going on and it was as though they waited for the verdict together.

'I'm opening it,' Stacey remarked.

'Are we divorced or still married?' she asked impatiently a few moments later.

'Still married.' Stacey's reply was clear and concise.

'We're still married,' Molly repeated, completely dazed.

CHAPTER SIX

MOLLY WAS STILL dazed as she sat at the table, once more allowing Fletch to move around her kitchen as though he lived there. He finished making both of them a soothing cup of herbal tea before sitting opposite her. She shook her head again. 'All these years. We've been married all these years.'

She sipped at her tea, relaxing a little at the soothing taste. 'We're still married.' The words were filled with incredulity and she looked across at Fletcher, watching him for a moment as he drank his tea.

'I know. Took me a while to wrap my head around everything.'

'So how did you?'

'How did I what?'

'Wrap your head around it.'

'Uh…well, I guess having time to process things does help.'

'And being the problem solver that you are, what conclusions have you come up with? I mean, do you just need to sign the papers or do we have to go through the whole rigmarole again?'

'We have to file again.'

'Right.' She sipped her tea. 'Would you mind if I used my own lawyer this time?'

He shook his head. 'No, but my cousins have offered to reprocess the documents at no cost, firmly assuring me that this time everything will go through just fine.'

'And we'll both open our letters when they arrive.'

He smiled at her then, his eyes filled with sorrow. 'Yes.'

Molly cradled her cup in her hands and thought things through. 'So what made you go looking for your divorce papers? Planning on remarrying?'

'Huh?' He stared at her as though she'd just guessed his guilty secret. 'Uh…how did you come to that conclusion?'

'Why else would you look at those papers after all this time? It's logical, Fletch.'

'I guess.' He sipped his tea. 'Basically, until we

get our divorce finalised, there's no moving on for either of us. Not legally, at any rate.'

'And emotionally?'

'Emotions always take longer to sort through, longer to process, longer to…forgive.'

Molly finished her tea and stood from the chair, walking to the sink. 'Are you asking me if I've forgiven you for what happened all those years ago?'

'Yes.'

She looked at him over her shoulder as she washed her cup and picked up a tea towel to dry it. 'We were both so young.'

'You've never wanted to get married again? Start a family?' She shook her head quickly. Now was not the time to think about children, about how scary it would be to feel a little human growing inside her again. She'd be worried throughout the entire pregnancy that something might happen to it, that she might do something wrong, that the baby would die.

Although everything had happened all those years ago, although the words Fletcher had said to her had been because he'd been feeling helpless and alone, and although she knew it hadn't been her fault, deep in the recesses of her mind, she knew she'd worry and stress throughout the entire pregnancy…*if* she was ever going to have children.

'I'm too busy trying to qualify,' she finally answered him. 'Besides, I have a big enough family already but clearly, given you're here, you do want to get married again.' She finished drying the cup and turned to put it away. 'So who's the lucky woman?'

Even though she and Fletcher had said their goodbyes so many years ago, there was still a stab of pain at the realisation that he was no longer available. Not to her, not to anyone…except—

'Eliza.' She looked at him again, seeing the surprise on his face at her accurate guess.

'How could you possibly know?'

'She's the only other woman you've mentioned since you arrived. Your fellowship tour manager, right? The one who's presently in Melbourne looking after her sick father?'

'Yes.'

'A nurse?'

'An ex-theatre sister.' He finished his tea and Molly immediately held out her hand for his cup, needing something to do. 'It was good having someone who understood the intricacies of surgery to plan the tour. She's a widow with one son.'

'Where's her son been while you've been travelling?' Molly didn't particularly want to know but, then again, Fletcher was her ex-husband...or soon would be. Why couldn't she be interested in his life, interested in making sure he was indeed happy because, above all, that was all she'd ever really wanted for him. She washed his cup and started to dry it.

'He's twenty years old.'

'Really?'

Fletcher nodded. 'He lives in Melbourne and is a second-year medical student.'

'Wow. She must have been young when she had him.'

'She was nineteen.' Fletcher looked at her, his tone soft and filled with compassion. Molly stopped drying the cup, a lump immediately forming in her throat. The memories she had to force herself to so often repress flooded to the fore of her thoughts. Irrational thoughts such as why Eliza's baby had lived but hers had died.

Why had *she* been the unlucky one? Why had her beautiful baby been taken from her?

She clenched her jaw in an effort to stop the tears that were pricking behind her eyes. Swallowing a few times, she sniffed and tried hard to control her wobbling lower lip.

'Oh, Molly.' Fletcher was beside her in an instant and took the tea towel and cup from her hands, placing them onto the bench before brushing her hair behind her ear and trailing his fingers down the side of her cheek. 'It still hurts?'

'It will *always* hurt.' The power behind her pain caused the floodgates to open and she started to cry. 'I know other women lose babies but…but…'

'Shh.' Fletcher drew her closer into his arms, wanting to offer some sort of comfort. He couldn't help but feel guilty at seeing her like this. It was his fault for the terrible way he'd handled things back then.

'And they all seem to get over it and move on with their lives but I…I…'

'Perhaps if we'd stayed together, perhaps if we'd tried for more children—' Fletcher stopped, knowing that no amount of 'what ifs' was going to change the past. It was clear to him that Molly still felt the loss of their beautiful baby girl with a great intensity, even after all these years.

'Did you ever speak to a counsellor about her?' he asked gingerly as he stroked her wayward curls, trying to ignore the way she felt in his arms. So perfect, so natural, so right.

'No. I just threw myself into my medical studies.'

'So did I.'

Molly sniffed and pulled back to look up at him. 'You did?'

'Sure. I'd lost the woman I loved and a baby girl all in one fell swoop and even though you eventually accepted my apology, it all came too late. We'd said too much.' He pulled a handkerchief from his pocket and dabbed at her eyes. 'My terrible temper, which I have spent years getting under better control, had made you hate me.'

'No. I've never hated you, Fletch.' She looked up at him with such a deep vulnerability, such a deep need, such a deep longing that he was having trouble fighting the urge to lower his mouth to hers and kiss her parted lips.

They'd stood in this exact position so many times in the past and even back then he'd thought her the most beautiful woman he'd ever seen. Nothing had changed. She was Molly. His Molly. Or…she had been.

When her tongue slipped out to wet her lips, her breathing having increased as much as his, he couldn't ignore the warning bells ringing in the back of his mind. She was so familiar and perfect and…Molly. She was the first woman he'd ever truly loved and he knew that love would never truly die.

'Is it serious?' Her whispered words filtered around him but his mind was too thick with desire that he didn't understand.

'Pardon?' He looked into her eyes, seeing her own need mirrored there. He stared for a long moment, all rational thought fleeing. 'You look the same.' The words sprang from his lips before he could stop them. 'Still so beautiful.' He swallowed and she watched the action of his Adam's apple moving up and down. She bit her lip and he knew of old that she wanted to slide her hands up his shoulders, stand on tiptoe and press tiny kisses to his exposed neck.

Fletcher closed his eyes, knowing he should push her away, knowing this wasn't right but unable to stop the emotions surging through him. Legally he had every right to follow his need but morally it was wrong.

'You shouldn't say such things if...you know... it's serious with...'

'Eliza.' He whispered the name of the woman who had filled his beige-coloured life with easy-going laughter. The problem was, Molly filled his world with Technicolor. He shouldn't compare the two. It wasn't fair to either of them, nor himself. Plus, Molly was seeing that Roger fellow so, technically, neither of them should be standing as they were, contemplating what they were contemplating.

Keeping his eyes still closed, he placed his hands at her hips and gently eased her away, exhaling slowly. When he looked at her, she'd crossed her arms over her chest, whether because she was cold or defensive, he wasn't sure. Perhaps it was both. 'Yes, it is...serious with Eliza.' He took three steps away from her and raked both hands through his hair. 'It's just that when I'm around you—' he shook his head in bemusement '—life as I know it seems to alter.'

'I understand.' Molly picked up the cup and tea

towel, finished drying the item and then put it back into the cupboard. It was clear she was uncomfortable, they both were, but Fletcher wasn't sure what he should do. Should he explain everything to Molly? Tell her all about Eliza and how, after working closely together, she'd asked him to marry her?

Should he tell her that when he'd gone searching for the divorce decree, needing that piece of paper so he and Eliza could begin the process of their own paperwork, he'd been assuaged with a plethora of memories he'd thought he'd put aside for ever? Should he tell her that when it had sunk in that he technically wasn't divorced, that he was in fact still married to Molly, a part of him had been ecstatically happy?

'I should go' was all he said.

'OK.' Her quick reply was indicative that she wanted him gone.

'I guess both of us have a lot to think through.'

'Yes.'

Monosyllables seemed to be all she was capable of now and he couldn't blame her. His own mind was a jumbled mess and as he turned and headed towards the front door she followed him.

'I can see myself out.' The sooner both of them were away from the uncomfortable atmosphere surrounding them, the better.

'OK.' She stopped in the doorway to the kitchen and waved. He nodded once, then opened her front door and slipped through, closing it behind him. Fletcher closed his eyes for a moment, unable to believe everything that had just happened. He'd almost kissed Molly! What had he been thinking?

'You weren't,' he mumbled as he pulled his keys from his pocket and quickly unlocked the door next to hers. 'What are you doing?' He walked towards his own kitchen, his duplex the mirror image of Molly's. 'You're supposed to tell her about the divorce, get her to sign the new papers and then you're out. Off with Eliza. Starting your new life!'

He closed his eyes and rested his head against the wall. 'And now you're talking to yourself.' He pulled out his cell phone and dialled Eliza's number. Talking to her would definitely help him to refocus, which was exactly what he needed. Eliza was calm and collected. She was relaxing and fun to be around. She didn't exasperate him, she didn't annoy him and she didn't make him forget everything else around him.

'Hello, you've reached Eliza. I'm unable to take your call at the moment, so please—' Fletcher groaned as he waited for her voicemail message to finish before leaving his message. He disconnected the call then went into the bedroom to lie down. Part of him was actually relieved Eliza hadn't answered as the sensation of guilt washed over him.

He'd almost kissed Molly!

Of course, he hadn't gone there with that intention; it had just happened. She'd been upset about Katie, their beautiful little baby girl, and seeing her like that had caused his own pain and regret to surface. All those years ago, he'd been on the other side of the country when she'd told him she'd lost the baby, that she'd gone into premature labour and that there had been complications. He hadn't handled the situation at all well. In fact, he'd been a downright brute. Even thinking about his behaviour back then turned his stomach and he wouldn't have blamed Molly if she'd never spoken to him again.

In his defence, he'd spent the prior week with

his squabbling, verbally abusive parents at a family wedding. Molly hadn't been able to fly across to Sydney with him given that she hadn't been feeling well throughout her pregnancy.

'It's best if I stay here in Perth,' she'd said. 'Close to my dad. If there's anything wrong with either me or the baby, I'll have the best GP in the world looking after me.'

Reluctantly, he'd agreed.

'Besides,' she'd continued as she'd folded his clothes neatly, helping him pack, 'from what you've told me about your family, I'm not sure I want to meet them.'

'My uncle and cousins aren't too bad, otherwise I wouldn't be going. I used to spend a lot of time with them on their farm when I was a teenager because my parents were too busy yelling at each other and drinking to even remember to feed me.'

'Sounds like a terrible childhood,' she'd said, coming to slip her arms around his waist, her baby bump pressing into his back. He'd looked at her over his shoulder before shifting so he could wrap his arms around her.

'It wasn't the best.'

'Why are your parents still together if they make each other so miserable?'

'I have no clue.' He'd kissed her, then bent to kiss her stomach. 'And when I get back,' he'd told the baby bump, 'Mummy and Daddy are going to have another talk about where we're going to live.'

Molly had sighed and turned away. 'Not this again. Fletch, I've told you. I can't have a baby and then move from Perth to the other side of Australia. I'll need my family around me, my sisters. Plus Cora still needs me.'

Fletcher could remember being fascinated at the bond the triplets shared but, being an only child, he'd never really understood it.

'I saw how much help Tish needed when Jasmine was born. The first year of motherhood is really difficult and plus half the time you'll be working a thousand hours at the hospital during your internship and I'll never see you. Then, when you finally get annual leave, you're planning to go overseas to work with Pacific Medical Aid.'

Fletcher had zipped up his suitcase and glared at her. 'You said you understood the need I have to do that type of work, to help others less fortunate, to ensure that medical care is available to everyone regardless of ethnicity or colour or gender.'

'Yes. I do understand and I think that's wonderful but what about me? What about my studies at medical school? Yes, I've been able to go part-time but once the baby's born, I'll need more help. I can't study and look after a baby and do the wifey things around the home without help.'

'We'll get you a nanny and a house cleaner.'

'That's not what I'm talking about.' She'd thrown her hands in the air and walked from the room. 'We've had this same argument on and off for months now.'

'Something's got to give.'

'Something or someone?' she'd asked, crossing her arms over her chest in defiance. When the car horn had beeped from outside their small apartment, she'd looked away. 'That's your taxi. Enjoy your five-hour flight and *family* wedding. Perhaps there you'll realise just how important family really is.'

'Don't I get a hug and a kiss goodbye?' he'd asked but she'd walked into the bathroom and shut the door. The taxi driver had beeped his horn again and Fletcher had had nothing else to do except to call, 'I love you,' to the apartment in general before heading out.

The family wedding had been a week-long affair at a fancy hotel situated on Sydney harbour. His uncle had spared no expense as his only daughter had been walked down the aisle and given away to some stockbroker Fletcher had never met.

Aunts and cousins and nephews and uncles and nieces had all gathered together and complained about each other behind backs but then had been all smiles and fake friendliness. His uncle, the father of the bride, had got rip-roaring drunk, confessing to Fletcher that his sons were trying to take over the law-firm business he'd built up from the ground, that they were trying to put him out to pasture.

Fletcher had murmured appropriate responses, then moved on to another table only to hear another relative moan about things while getting sloshed. When his mother had berated his father because his father had dared to grope one of the waitresses, the gathered family had cheered. The verbal abuse, the emotional bullying, the hatred, had pierced through him.

He had known Molly's family was different, that they loved and supported each other, but did she really want to live on the other side of the country from her husband? Then, when she'd called him on the phone, completely distraught, and told him that she'd gone into premature labour and their daughter hadn't been able to make it, Fletch had been shocked.

'What on earth were you doing that made you go into premature labour?' The nasty abuse from spending time with his extended family had bled into his words, infecting him. 'Did you drink something? Eat something? Did you go on another long walk with Stacey?'

'Fletch—I didn't *do* anything.'

'Clearly. Otherwise you would have realised something was wrong and gone to the hospital earlier. I thought your father was looking after you. The best GP in the world. Hah. You'd have been better off coming with me to Sydney. At least there are better hospitals here.'

'Fletch.' She'd sobbed down the phone line but his grief had been fuelled by anger.

'That's it, Molly. As your husband I'm putting my foot down. You're moving to Sydney with me. No more arguments.'

'Fletcher...' The tears had continued. 'I don't understand why...why...'

'I'll rent a place while I'm here and then when I get back, we're packing up and moving over here before the month is out.'

'She's dead, Fletcher. Can't you hear me? Our little Katie, our baby girl—she's...she's...'

'You *named* her without me? We hadn't decided on names. That does it. I'm booking a flight home right now. See you tonight.'

With that, he'd slammed down the phone.

Even now, Fletch still cringed at his behaviour back then. His young wife had needed him and he hadn't been able to be there for her due to his own selfish emotions. He'd never shared deep-seated pain before, always going it alone when things went wrong. He hadn't known how to support Molly while still holding himself together. What he should have done was to stay with her, to grieve with her, to cry with her for their loss.

'Katie.' It was a beautiful name and he couldn't understand why he'd been so angry at her. She'd

done what she'd had to do. He knew that now.
'Hindsight.' He shook his head, wishing he could
go back and do things all over again but that was
impossible.

CHAPTER SEVEN

WHEN MOLLY WOKE the next morning, she couldn't believe how exhausted she felt. The past few days had been incredibly hectic and then yesterday evening, discovering that she was still married to Fletcher and then crying about Katie and learning that Fletcher was involved with another woman and that it was serious and—

She shifted in the bed, realising she was lying on something lumpy. She pulled out whatever it was only to discover it was Katie's teddy bear. Molly hugged the bear tight. Her sisters had bought this bear for the new addition to their family.

'I don't care if it's a boy or a girl,' Cora had stated. 'This baby is going to be absolutely smothered with aunty love.' She'd just come home from a short stay in hospital due to a kidney infection. After having her pelvis crushed in a horrendous car accident and thus having surgery to remove one of her ovaries, Cora had been told by her doctors that she would never be able to naturally carry a child, which made Molly's little baby all that more precious to the three of them.

'From both of us,' Stacey had added as she'd smoothed the red satin bow tied delicately around the teddy bear's neck.

'I think Jasmine might be the one to smother her with aunty love,' Molly had added, the three of them laughing as the one-and-a-half-year-old toddler had come running into the room, begging to be picked up.

Molly had cuddled her little sister close, imagining what it might be like to do that with her own child. 'What shall we call the bear?' she'd asked Jasmine.

'Katie.' Jasmine's little voice had spoken the word clearly.

'I like Katie.' Molly had nodded.

'Me, too,' Stacey had added.

'I like it as well but I like it for the baby, not the teddy bear.' Cora's words had been thoughtful and positive. 'Not Kate, not Kathryn or Kath but Katie.'

'Katie Thompson.' Molly had grinned as she'd said the name, nodding. 'When Fletch gets back to Perth, I'll run it by him.'

'How's things going at his family's wedding reunion thing?' Stacey had accepted a wriggling Jasmine from Molly.

'Not good. He rarely sees his parents and mentioned that, after this wedding, he'd be more than happy never to see them again.'

'I guess we just don't understand.' Cora had held her hands out for a cuddle with Jasmine.

'No.' Molly had sighed. 'And that's why Fletcher doesn't seem to understand that I can't leave here to go and live on the other side of Australia without my sisters.'

'It's difficult for anyone who isn't a twin or a triplet to understand the bond we share. It's not just that we're sisters, it's that we're connected,' Stacey had added, handing Katie's bear to Molly.

Molly looked at the faded red ribbon with its slightly frayed edges, remembering all the times she'd cuddled that teddy bear whenever she hadn't been able to sleep, whenever she'd been plagued with memories of her past, of Fletcher and their beautiful little girl.

She kissed the bear and put it from her, knowing she needed to get up. Her alarms hadn't gone off yet so thankfully she had plenty of time to take things easy this morning. Having Fletcher burst back into her life, it was little wonder that so many old memories were beginning to surface.

As she turned over she checked the clock and did a double take when she saw the time. 'What?' How had she slept through her alarms? Ward round would be starting in ten minutes' time. As though on cue, her phone rang, the crazy ringtone she'd assigned to Alexis piercing the silence of her room.

'Where are you?' Alexis asked as Molly connected the call.

'I'm coming. I'm coming. I overslept.'

'Were you called in last night? Did something happen I don't know about?'

'I'll be there as soon as I can,' Molly replied.

'OK. I'll let Fletcher know.'

'Why should *he* need to know?' Molly retorted as she tried to climb out of the bed but in her haste ended up with her feet tangled in the sheets.

'He's taking ward round this morning.'

'Is he there?'

'He's been here since just before six o'clock. Said he couldn't sleep so he's been catching up on the cases he's going to review.'

'That's just perfect,' she mumbled. Her not-ex-husband was taking ward round on the only morning that she was late! Always the way. 'I'll be there as soon as I can,' she repeated and disconnected the call, now desperately trying to kick her feet free, absolutely hating the sensation of being unable to move. It was part of who she was. Always needing to have a certain amount of freedom. Perhaps it was because she was one of three that she wanted to assert her independence, even if it was in small ways. Cora and Stacey called it her Mollyness.

'It's what makes you Molly.' Cora had laughed.

'Our Mad Molly,' Stacey had added, the three of them giggling together.

It was why she'd decided to pursue surgery, why she'd moved to Sydney and why, all those years ago, she'd impulsively married Fletcher. She didn't like being told she couldn't do something, she didn't like other people organising her life, as Fletch had tried to do after they were married, and she didn't like being restrained, thus the bed sheets ended up in a complete mess on the floor, Molly taking her frustrations out on them.

She quickly dressed in navy trousers and a light blue shirt, then tamed her hair back into a bun, lacquering the sides into place. She felt austere and aloof, wanting her outward appearance to reflect that.

Quickly grabbing her keys, hospital key card and bag, Molly pulled the front door closed behind her and headed off for the hospital at a brisk pace. She could grab a coffee and something to eat at the first available opportunity, which would hopefully be between ward round and the meeting she was scheduled to attend at nine-thirty.

'How could you have slept in? So unprofessional,' she chastised herself in a mumbled whisper. All she could concentrate on now was getting to work as fast as possible and hoping that she could just slip onto the end of the round without being noticed. Ha! Of course he'd notice. She was his *wife*.

The squeal of tyres up ahead stopped her thoughts dead, a sickening feeling rolling in her stomach, which had nothing to do with the fact that she hadn't eaten anything for breakfast. She stopped walking and listened...waited. Time seemed to stand still, to freeze but then, when she heard the sound of metal upon metal, of people screaming, of more squealing tyres, the world around her seemed to jump into fast forward.

Molly ran towards where the sounds were coming from, the cries for help guiding her in the right direction. She pulled her cell phone from her pocket, dialling Alexis's cell phone. 'Hi. I'm going to be much later than originally expected,' she said before Alexis could talk. 'Motor vehicle accident, one block up from the hospital. No doubt people have already called the emergency number.'

'Where are you exactly?' Alexis asked, concern in her tone.

'Just crossing the road.' Molly scanned the area. 'There's a bus in the middle of the road, two cars have been hit but it looks as though they were parked. Not sure if there are any occupants of the vehicles.' She continued to describe what she was seeing as she moved closer. 'One person on the road. Not moving. Looks like a teenage boy.' She stopped running and walked briskly through the people who were gathering around, some of them covering their mouths, unsure what to do or how to react to the trauma they were seeing. 'Bus driver appears unconscious.' She pushed her way through the few people who were around the teenager. 'I'm a doctor,' she told them briskly, her no-nonsense tone brooking no argument.

Molly pressed her fingers to the teenager's carotid pulse. 'Pulse is there but thready.'

'The calls have come in,' Alexis informed her, then Molly could hear her friend muttering something to someone else. 'Sister's on the hospital phone letting the paramedic crews know that you're already on site.'

'OK.' Molly turned her attention to her patient. 'Can you hear me?' she called to the teenager.

'Is there any response?'

Molly actually pulled the phone from her ear and looked at it. It wasn't Alexis on the other end but Fletcher.

'Molly? Molly?'

'I'm here,' she remarked, trying to instil polite professionalism into her tone. It didn't matter what was happening between them; their private lives had nothing whatsoever to do with this situation. She checked the teenager's pulse again. At least he was breathing. She called to him.

'I'm Dr Wilton. Can you hear me?' She received a murmur; there was no coherence to his words. 'Mild response,' she remarked into the phone.

'That's something. Is he stable enough for you to check the rest of the area so we have a better idea of what we might find?'

'Not really. Just a second.' Molly looked around and it was then she saw a woman in her sixties running towards her.

'I'm a retired nurse,' the woman said as she drew closer to Molly, a little out of breath.

'Great. Can you go and check on cars over there and give me a report?'

'Done.' The woman headed off and Molly lifted the phone from her ear. 'I'm going to put you on speaker,' she told Fletch and put the phone on the ground so she had two hands to work with. 'I just want to check his injuries.' Very carefully, she shifted around the teenager, needing to get a better look. 'Ribs feel gone on the right side, decreased air intake.'

'Blunt force trauma. Do you think he might have been struck by the bus or one of the cars?'

'Given his height and the position of the injuries, I'd go with the bus.' She kept carefully checking her patient. 'Right femur and left tibia and fibula feel fractured.' She felt his ankle for a pulse. 'No blood loss and weak pulse in his ankle.'

'So we can assume femoral artery is intact.'

The patient made a sound again and Molly spoke to him. 'I'm Dr Wilton,' she said again. 'Stay still. Help is on the way.'

The retired nurse came running back, puffing. 'Two adults in the car, one female, one male. Both appear to be unconscious but a woman's been hit by their car. She's under the front tyre. She's dead.'

Molly closed her eyes for a moment and took a breath, shoving this sad news to the back of her mind. She opened her eyes with focus and purpose. She looked up at the nurse. 'What's your name?'

'Vreni.'

'I'm Molly. We need to get this boy stabilised.'

She directed her words to the phone. 'Fletch, how long before support arrives?'

'We'll be there in two, possibly three minutes,' Fletcher replied and it sounded as though he was moving briskly.

That stopped her for a second. '*You're* coming?'

'Alexis, myself and the rest of the recovery crew are climbing into the ambulance now,' he told her. 'Keep the line open.'

'Vreni, can you stay with him? See if you can get a better response from him but, most of all, keep his head stable. I'm going to try taking a closer look at the bus driver.'

'OK.'

Molly picked up the phone and took it with her. It wasn't until she reached the back door of the bus that she realised there were passengers inside. They were trying to get the rear door open, the three of them looking rather panicked as the emergency door release seemed to be jammed.

'You may need to try the rear window,' she called to them, pointing to the back of the bus where the emergency window was located. 'Lie on the seat and kick the window with your feet. Do it at the same time,' she called to them. The sound of sirens filled the air. Molly knew that within a matter of ten minutes all the emergency services, fire, ambulance and police, would be on the scene and she would have assistance but for now, if she could get these people out of the back of the bus, she could attempt to get in that way and take a closer look at the driver.

Thankfully, the passengers all worked in unison and were soon climbing out of the rear window.

'Go and sit over there on the kerb,' she instructed them. The morning traffic had now slowed to a crawl and down to one lane, the commuters stopping to stare at the emergency for as long as possible. 'Where are you?' she asked Fletcher as she put the phone in her pocket.

'Working our way through the traffic. Give us another two minutes.'

'Just as well I used to do gymnastics when I was little,' she commented as she finished climbing into the bus. 'Driver looks as though he's trapped, quite badly. Hello? Can you hear me?' she asked. 'I'm Dr Wilton. What's your name?'

'Jerry,' he managed to say, his breathing uneven.

'OK, Jerry.' She felt his pulse. 'Just keep real still for me.'

'I can't move my legs.'

'Right. Let me see if I can have a look,' she said, bending down to carefully shift a bit of the dashboard that seemed to have curled around the driver's legs. She took the phone out of her pocket and spoke to Fletcher. 'Are you still there, Fletch?'

'I'm not going anywhere,' he told her and at the moment she was extremely comforted by his words.

'Driver has sustained an injury to his legs. I can't shift the debris but I can see beneath it. Part of the steering wheel has broken off and is lodged in his upper thigh. Other than that, he's stable for now so long as he stays still.' She stood and put her hand on Jerry's shoulder. 'You're going to stay nice and still for me, aren't you?' she said with a smile in her words.

'Whatever you say, doc,' he replied.

'That's good news. I need to leave you now but crews will be here soon.'

'We can't get through any further at the moment. Cars are banked up,' Fletch told her. 'I'm climbing from the transport now and bringing the kit with me. We'll probably need the helicopter to lift the patients out.'

'Get Alexis to sort that out,' Molly stated as Jerry told her where to find the emergency lever to open the front doors of the bus. This she did and, with the phone still to her ear, she returned to where Vreni was monitoring the teenage boy.

'I can see you,' Fletch called and within the next second he'd hung up. Molly looked in the distance and saw him running towards her, dressed in bright retrieval overalls with the word 'Doctor' emblazoned on the back and front.

Molly shoved her phone back into her pocket and looked to Vreni. 'Any change?' she asked.

'His breathing is still raspy but he's managed to tell me his name. It's Davis.'

'Hello, Davis. I'm Dr Wilton. We're going to get you all sorted out now.'

Within another moment, Fletcher was kneeling down beside her, opening the large medical backpack to retrieve some gloves. He handed some to Vreni and to Molly, the paramedics coming alongside them and carefully stabilising Davis's head and neck in a brace.

Molly took a stethoscope from the bag and immediately listened to Davis's breathing. 'His air
intake is definitely decreased on the left side.'

'Pelvis is unstable, pulse is still good in both
legs,' Fletcher remarked as he ran his hands over
Davis's lower injuries, checking them. 'Let's get
a drip into him and some pain relief. Pass me the
portable monitor,' he stated to another one of the
paramedics. Together they worked to hook Davis
to the monitor that gave them an ECG read-out
as well as monitoring his blood pressure and
oxygen saturations.

By the time they were done, Molly looked up
and it was then she finally became aware of the
other emergency crews. The fire-brigade crews
were busy cutting away the driver's side window of the bus to allow the paramedics easier
access to both sides of the driver. Alexis was
with Jerry, helping to stabilise him. Several of
the other paramedics and emergency doctors
were with the passengers of the car and she saw
the one police officer covering the deceased
woman's body with a blanket until they were
able to successfully move her to a more suitable
resting place.

'OK,' Fletch remarked as he monitored Davis's output. 'He should be OK to stretcher and move. How long until the helicopter arrives?' He asked the last question to the paramedic, who immediately pulled out his two-way radio to confirm these details.

Just after they'd successfully transferred Davis to the stretcher, one of the paramedics using a bag to ensure Davis received enough oxygen, the portable machine that was monitoring his vital signs began beeping.

'Sats are falling,' Molly remarked.

Fletch immediately hooked a stethoscope into his ears and listened to Davis's breathing. 'He's going bradycardic.'

'Pressure's going down,' Vreni said.

'All signs are pointing to tamponade,' Molly added.

'We're going to need to open him up and find where he's bleeding,' Fletcher stated firmly.

'Here?' Vreni stared at him as though he were completely insane. 'On the street? He might die.'

'If we don't try, then he'll definitely die,' Fletcher remarked, pulling different pieces of equipment from the medical kit. He looked to the paramedics. 'I need lung spreaders and a full surgical kit, stat.'

One of the paramedics headed off to fulfil the request. 'We're going to need some screens around the patient,' Molly said to a nearby police officer. Within a matter of minutes, Fletcher was ready to proceed with the emergency surgery.

He looked at Molly, his blue gaze intense but filled with absolute confidence. She drew strength from that. 'Ready to do a thoracotomy?'

She nodded once. 'Ready.'

'Scalpel,' he said and she placed it into his hand. He made a neat incision on the left side of Davis's chest, Vreni ensuring that the teenager's left arm was out of the way above his head. Molly had the blunt scissors ready for when Fletcher needed to cut through the muscle tissue. They inserted the spreaders, which gave them a bigger area to find out what was causing Davis to fail. The paramedic was still squeezing the bag with a regular rhythm so that Davis's lungs received oxygen. Vreni was supplying gauze and packing to mop up the blood surrounding the wound, trying to keep it as clear as possible. 'Feel around, Molly. See if you can locate that bleeder.'

She did as she was told. 'Found a clot. There's a hole in the right atrium.' She held out her hand. 'Clamp.'

Vreni reached into the surgical kit and quickly handed Molly a clamp.

'Careful. It's as thin as tissue paper,' Fletcher stated as he carefully cut through the pericardium to reach the heart. He went to reach in to massage the heart but stopped.

'I'm on the wrong angle and my hands are too big.' He took the clamp from Molly and she immediately put her hand around Davis's heart.

'Quality massage but don't kink it. Keep it level,' he reported. After a few moments, when there was still no output, he shook his head.

'I'm going to give him some adrenaline.' He pulled a shot of adrenaline from the emergency medical kit and inserted the needle straight into the heart.

'Still nothing,' Molly said, trying desperately to keep the concern from her voice.

Fletcher flicked the heart. Nothing. He flicked the heart again and this time Davis's body responded but not in the way they'd hoped.

'Hmm, not bossy but perhaps…direct. Sometimes too direct,' he clarified softly.

'Oh, please. Not now. I'm too exhausted to take another trip down memory lane.'

'I know.'

Molly closed her eyes and listened to him moving around the room, making her a coffee.

'Here you are.' His voice was soft and caring and she knew she'd missed him far more than she'd allowed herself to admit. Just having him near her, his comforting presence, his support. She accepted the coffee with thanks and sipped from the cup.

'Ah.'

'Better?'

'Oh, yes.'

They sat in a comfortable silence for a while, not needing to talk. It was nice. Reassuring. Wonderful.

'It wasn't all bad,' she finally murmured.

'There was a lot of good,' he agreed, knowing she wasn't referring to the events of the morning but rather the events of their past.

Her phone beeped, breaking the bubble around them. She checked the message.

'It's Alexis. They've arrived with the bus driver,' she told him, her tone flat.

Fletcher stood and drank his coffee down. 'Back to work we go.' He forced a smile as he accepted Molly's empty cup and washed it before opening the door for her.

She looked up at him and nodded, trying desperately not to focus on his delightful mouth so very close to her own. She had to keep reminding herself that Fletcher now belonged to someone else, and also that she was seeing Roger.

Why was her life so complicated all of a sudden?

The answer was the man who walked beside her, the man she knew she would never stop loving—ever.

CHAPTER EIGHT

IT WAS ONE of those odd days where nothing seemed to go as planned, but such was the life of a surgeon. Clinics and theatre lists could be planned in advance but when an emergency came in, everything else had to get shuffled.

The junior registrars and interns did as much as they could in clinic but all of them, especially the interns, were eager to do as much surgical time as possible.

'We only had to reappoint ten patients,' the out-patient sister told her later that afternoon when Molly stopped by for a recap. 'Everyone else was seen...eventually.'

'That's not too bad.'

'How's that young teenage boy? I heard you performed a thoracotomy in the street.'

Molly smiled. 'The patient's doing very well now and I didn't perform the surgery. I only assisted Fletcher.' She stopped and looked down at the ground, smiling a little as she remembered just how confident and assured Fletch had been whilst performing a very difficult procedure. 'I guess all that experience in the middle of no-where has definitely paid off because Fletcher was incredible.'

Sister nodded and Molly stretched her arms before drawing in a deep breath. 'What's next?' Sister asked.

'Off to the ward to check on the patients.' She waved goodbye to Sister and headed towards the surgical wards. Right at this moment, she had to admit that she was happy. The patients from this morning's tragedy, except for the woman who had died at the scene, were all alive and, with time, should make a full recovery. But it wasn't only her patients who were making her happy and she knew exactly what—or rather *who*—was responsible for her present mood.

'Heading to the ward?'

'Fletcher.' She stopped and looked over her shoulder to see him behind her. 'Where are you coming from?'

'The hospital director's office. He wanted

to personally thank me for my assistance with today's emergency.'

'Well, that's nice.' They both started walking again and for some reason, Molly's fingers itched to be holding firmly onto his. He really was such a clever man. Not many surgeons would have been able to pull off such an operation, especially in those circumstances. She was proud of him.

'Actually, I think it was more of a publicity thing.'

'Oh?'

'Prestigious doctor, research fellow. Pacific Medical Aid surgeon saves teenage boy's life on the side of the road.' He lifted his hand as though he were highlighting tomorrow's newspaper headlines.

'Not very catchy. Plus, it will definitely inflate your ego far more than it already is. Ooh, when the journalist gets here, you could do some magic tricks for the camera. Everybody loves magic.'

Fletch chuckled and draped his arm about her shoulders—just as a close friend would. 'There's the sassy Molly I adore.' He winked at her and then dropped his arm, pressing the button for the door to allow them into the surgical ward.

It felt wonderful to joke and tease with him again. It felt natural and right and her smile increased even more. Maybe they could find a level of friendship they were both comfortable with. They headed towards Ward Sister for an updated report before completing a quick and very belated ward round then heading up to the paediatric intensive care unit to check on Davis. The passengers of the parked car that the bus had crashed into were being kept in the medical ward overnight for observation but were otherwise fine.

Davis's mother sat by his bedside, looking ashen and scared. Molly headed over and put her hand on the woman's shoulder. 'Hello. I'm Molly Wilton and this is Fletcher Thompson. We met after Davis came out of surgery.'

'Oh. Oh, yes.' The woman smiled vaguely at Molly. 'Sorry. You look different out of your theatre clothes.'

'Can I get you a drink of something?' Fletcher asked.

'No. No.' She returned her attention to watching her son lying there, no doubt looking so very different. 'He looks so small and yet so grown up all at the same time.'

'His vital signs are excellent,' Fletch told her softly. 'It's going to be a long and bumpy road for a while but, in time, there's no reason why Davis shouldn't make a full recovery.'

'Do you know what happened? The police said he was hit by a bus but that they'd know more when he regained consciousness and they could question him further. Is that right because it sounds so…unreal?'

'His injuries are certainly consistent with some-one who has been struck by a vehicle,' Fletch explained. 'But beyond that, it'll be up to the crash investigation team to piece together exactly what happened.'

'For now,' Molly said, smiling encouragingly at the distraught mother, 'just concentrate on the fact that Davis is doing very well. The nursing staff have our phone numbers if you need to talk to us or to clarify things.'

'We'll be around to see him in the morning,' Fletcher remarked as they headed to CCU to see Jerry. With his profusely bleeding leg, it was a wonder they'd been able to save him as well as his limb.

'Is it true that if the accident had happened further away from the hospital, I'd be dead?' Jerry asked, his words slow and slurred.

Fletch glanced at Molly, both silently communicating with how to answer this rather sticky question. Playing the 'what if' game when you'd just come through a major trauma was nothing new but the last thing Jerry needed now was to speculate on what might have been.

'But it didn't. You're here. You're patched up and before you know it, you'll be heading home to your wife.'

'Hmm.' Jerry frowned. 'She's going to put me on another diet, be even more fussy about my cholesterol intake and bug me to exercise more.'

'Well, if it's any help, the physiotherapists who'll be around to see you tomorrow morning will be starting the same chant.' Molly smiled at Jerry's groan. 'Watch what you eat and start gentle exercises.' She placed her hand on Jerry's shoulder. 'I think you're going to do just fine.'

'And it's all thanks to you and your teams.' Jerry's smile dimmed as he stared at both Molly and Fletcher. 'Alexis has already been to see me and now you two. The people here really care about their patients. It's…it's humbling. Makes me want to be a better person.'

'I like it when patients say things like that,' Molly remarked after they'd said goodbye to Jerry and left the ICU.

'Gives you a sense of accomplishment,' Fletcher added. They both collected their jackets and bags from the surgical lockers then headed out of the hospital.

'I presume it's OK for me to walk you home?'

Molly grinned up at him. 'Well, given we live next door to each other, I can hardly stop you.'

He was very pleased with this answer and as they walked along he was hard pressed not to put his arm about her shoulders, just as he'd used to. 'Mr Majors is doing exceptionally well,' he commented and she agreed, the two of them discussing their patient for a minute or two.

'He's a bright character, isn't he? Always excited and happy. It's rare to see people happy when they're in hospital,' she said.

'Except if you're in the paediatric ward and the clown patrol is out to make your day.'

'The clown patrol and visiting magician,' she

pointed out. 'Do you do jungle magic when you're in Tarparnii?'

He laughed at her question but shook his head. 'Just normal magic.'

'Do you remember Paris?' she asked and Fletcher immediately smiled.

'Lots of magic there—but of a different kind.' He grinned. 'Are you talking about the Eiffel Tower or Louvre?'

She laughed. 'Both were equal disasters but I'm referring to what happened outside the Louvre. Your French certainly could have done with a brush-up before you opened your mouth.'

'Was it my fault I mangled things up a bit?'

'Yes. If it wasn't for the fact that the man spoke English, you could have been locked up for wanting to buy illegal drugs.'

'All I wanted was to buy you some flowers.' He chuckled and scratched his head. 'Still not sure how I got so confused.' He paused on the front porch and reached for her hand. He brought it to his lips and kissed it. 'Go and have a quiet night. Sleep sweet.'

'You're not going to attempt to talk your way in and offer to cook food for me?'

He shook his head, giving her that slow, small smile that often set her heart racing. 'Not to-night.'

'OK.'

They stood there looking at each other, the tension increasing between them. The undeni-able attraction—the one that had started so long ago—was still clearly present and all she wanted was for him to step forward and kiss her. She wanted to forget all about their past, to pretend that they'd just met, that they were dating, that they belonged together for ever.

'So…what now? I mean, what happens next?' she asked softly, still staring up into his hypnotic blue eyes. Neither of them was showing any sign of wanting to leave, of wanting to part.

'Uh…' He swallowed, trying to think clearly but it was difficult when her tantalising scent was winding its way about him. 'What happens next?' He knew the answer to this question but it took a while for him to filter through the sensual fog surrounding them. 'With us?' He clarified.

'Yes.' He'd only be here until the end of next week and he was really hoping that they'd be able to cement some sort of friendship so that afterwards, when he left and went back to Eliza, they could at least keep in touch.

'Well, I'll be needing that piece of paper from the lawyer, just for confirmation. Can you get Stacey to send it?'

'Sure. Sure.' She blinked, the enticing atmosphere beginning to dissipate. 'Actually, I'm heading to Newcastle this weekend, so I could pick it up then and give it to you on Monday.'

He nodded. 'Sounds good.' Still he didn't move, just stared at her for a moment. 'Or I could come to Newcastle with you? See your sisters again? Meet your other siblings?'

She was surprised at the suggestion but quickly answered, not wanting him to change his mind. Fletch wanted to come away with her for the weekend? 'Er...can you take the time?'

'I don't have any work planned except to keep an eye on Mr Majors and plan for Alexis's surgical procedure.'

'And you want to come to Newcastle with me?' she clarified.

'If that's all right? Would Stacey mind?'

'No. Not at all, and you'll be able to catch up

with everyone. Stacey and Cora and their hus-
bands.'

'What did you say Cora's husband's name was?'

'Archer. Archer Wild.' Molly raised her eyebrows. 'Do you know him?'

'Yeah, I do.' He smiled, now looking forward
even more to spending a few days in Newcastle.
'We've worked together in Tarparnii many times
before.'

'Of course. Archer practically grew up there.'

'Haven't seen him in years. Wow. He's married
to Cora?' He shook his head. 'It's a small world.'

'It certainly is.' The fact that the two of them
were standing here proved it. 'So we're on, then?'
She raised her eyebrows in question. 'Drive down
to Newcastle on Friday night, drive back Sunday
evening?'

'It's less than a two-hour drive now, isn't it?'

'Oh, yes.' She giggled. 'It *is* a long time since
you've been back. We can hire a car.'

'I'll take care of that.' He pulled his house keys
from his pocket and she followed suit. 'The weekend is only two days away and I have a lot of
preparation to do for my lecture first thing in
the morning.'

'OK.' Molly opened her door and grinned at him. 'Goodnight...Fetching Fletcher.' As she stepped into her place she heard his warm, rich laughter ring out, making her own smile increase. She leaned against the wall, wanting so desperately to return to him, to throw herself into his arms. After all, she rationalised, they were still legally husband and wife.

That thought, however, was enough to sober her wayward emotions. They *were* husband and wife—and Fletcher was with someone else. Molly knew that by ignoring the past she was probably setting herself up for a mound of heartbreak but just being with Fletcher and having fun with Fletcher and flirting with Fletcher was exciting and thrilling and a whole host of other delightful emotions she hadn't felt in so very long.

'You're playing a dangerous game with him,' Stacey said later when Molly called her to check it was all right for her to bring Fletcher home.

'But it's an exciting game,' replied Cora. It was how it had always been. Stacey was the sensible one and Cora was the adventurous one. Molly had always thought she was the mad, mischievous one but lately she was starting to question that. Studying surgery left her little time for dancing and going out and doing all the things she used to love to do. At least she was able to participate in the clown patrol and, of course, her recent dates with Roger had certainly brushed away a few cobwebs.

'What are you going to do about Roger?' Stacey asked as though she could read Molly's thoughts.

'The sexy physician,' Cora added with a purr, making them all laugh.

'There's nothing going on between Fletcher and myself other than two friends reconnecting.'

'And signing divorce papers,' Stacey pointed out.

'And that.' Molly frowned. 'But—'

'But you know what you have to do,' Stacey continued. 'You can't string Roger on, not when you feel that way about Fletcher.'

Molly knew there was no use denying it, especially when Roger had left a message on her voicemail, asking her out for a celebratory drink after her surgery, and Molly's text-message reply had been to simply say she was too tired.

'He's certainly fun to be around,' she told her

sisters, 'but I just can't picture myself sitting on the lounge, watching a movie with him.'

'He's been good for you in the sense that he's made you actually leave your place, to go out and socialise with others, to have a bit of fun,' Cora pointed out.

'But perhaps your "going out and being the life of the party" days are over,' Stacey added. Molly pondered her sisters' words, knowing they weren't being mean but more matter-of-fact. 'We'll be thirty-five soon.'

'Grown-ups,' Molly agreed.

'But what about Fletcher?' Cora wanted to know.

'Fletcher's with someone else. I can accept that,' Molly answered. 'And I hope we can be friends but with regards to Roger, you're right. It's a dead-end relationship and Roger definitely deserves to find someone else to have fun with.'

'Breaking it off with Roger?' Cora asked.

'Breaking it off with Roger,' Molly confirmed. That way at least her own conscience would be clear when she teased and laughed with Fletcher.

'You like flirting with Fletcher,' Stacey stated.

'It's natural because you know each other so well. Just…be careful.'

'Of course. I'm always careful because I have the two of you—'

'Watching my back,' the three of them said in unison.

'Love you, sis. See you in two sleeps' time.'

Molly ended the Internet chat session and, as it was still quite early, she called Roger, letting him know the situation.

'We were always casual,' he told her. 'But I completely understand. We can still be friends, right?'

'Definitely. Friends sounds good. Thanks, Roger.'

With a clear conscience, Molly made herself a light dinner and, for the first time since he'd moved in next door, purposely listened for signs of Fletcher moving about. When he'd first arrived a few days ago, she'd been aware of every move he made, but now as she listened she couldn't hear anything.

When she went to bed, she ensured her alarm was set and closed her eyes. Tonight she wasn't going to try to stop the wonderful memories of the times she'd spent with Fletcher from infiltrating her dreams, and as she lay there she could well remember the way they'd walked hand in hand along the Seine, and how they'd gazed in wonder at the pyramids in Egypt and how they'd played the roulette wheel in Las Vegas before running off to the chapel to get married.

'Are we doing the right thing?' Molly had laughed as they'd both stood in the waiting area of the small wedding chapel.

'Yes.' Fletcher's answer had been filled with determination and love. 'I have never felt about anyone the way I feel about you, Molly.' He'd kissed her, the feel of his lips on hers helping to give her courage. 'Besides, what was it your sister said?'

Molly's smile had increased. 'Stacey said that I was insane but that this was just the sort of thing that I would do.'

'Because you're fun loving…' He'd kissed one cheek. 'Adorable.' He'd kissed the other. 'Vivacious.' He'd kissed her nose before gazing deeply into her eyes. 'And so incredibly perfect for me.' He'd kissed her lips again, slowly, tenderly, letting her see that he was as much in love with her as she was with him. He'd rested his forehead against hers, his tone soft. 'And what did Cora say?'

It had taken a moment for Molly to get her thoughts back into a level of coherence as every fibre of her being had been zinging with delight at the seductive way Fletcher had just kissed her. 'She, er...she said that life is for living,' Molly had whispered. 'To take those chances of happiness when you find them.'

'And she's right.'

'She's survived a major accident,' Molly had agreed.

'Which means she knows what she's talking about.'

'Absolutely.' Molly had stood on tiptoe and wrapped her arms about his neck, her fingers playing with the ends of his hair, which had been long enough to touch the edge of his shirt collar. She'd kissed him again, allowing the sensations of their combined love to surround her. He'd been *her* Fletch. It hadn't mattered that they'd only known each other for a few short weeks, when you knew—you just *knew*.

'Next? Uh...Miss Molly Wilton and Mr Fletcher

Thompson?' At the sound of their names being called, Fletcher had reluctantly drawn back from his bride-to-be.

'*Dr* Fletcher Thompson,' Molly had corrected the woman who had already taken their details and their money.

'Ah...' He'd grinned at her. 'So you're just marrying me because I'm a doctor, eh?' Molly had rolled her eyes but laughed with him as they'd entered the chapel, both of them ready to make their vows to each other.

'This is for ever,' he'd declared, looking directly into her eyes as he'd slid the wedding ring into place. 'I love you, Molly.'

She sighed and hugged the pillow close to her, the dream washing over her with such perfect clarity that it felt as though the events had taken place just yesterday. 'Fletch.' His name was a whispered caress into the dark and as she shifted in the bed, wishing he still lay beside her, her mind drifted off into another dream.

Fletch carrying his new wife over the threshold of their hotel room. Fletch sitting next to her on the plane ride back to Perth, holding her hand in his or letting her rest her head on his shoulder and sleep. Fletch meeting her family for the first time, unable to believe how welcoming and inclusive they all were.

'I thought your father at least would have been angry with you. He didn't exactly give his approval when you spoke to him on the phone,' he'd told her as they'd headed to the bedroom Molly's stepmother had set up for them.

'He's my dad. He loves me. Faults and all.'

'Really? I didn't know that sort of love existed…at least, until I met you.' He'd kissed her and held her tight, Molly wondering whether there would ever come a time when she wouldn't want his arms around her. She hadn't been able to even contemplate that.

'Fletch. We need to work at this,' she'd told him a few nights later as they'd allowed the soft sea breeze from the Indian ocean to wash over them, cooling them down.

'I know. Marriage isn't easy. I've had daily proof of that for most of my life. My parents hate each other.'

'You're joking?' Molly had snuggled closer to him, her tone radiating disbelief and that Fletch really was teasing her.

'No.'

It was then she'd heard the pain in his voice and she'd shifted, raising herself up onto her elbow to look at him. 'Really? They hate each other?'

'Yes. I have no idea why they've stayed together all these years. Probably to keep making each other miserable,' he'd muttered and closed his eyes.

'Surely they must love each other deep down inside, otherwise they would have divorced.'

'My mother has refused to grant my father a divorce, even though he's had several affairs.'

'What?' Molly had been completely stunned. 'Er…I mean I know some marriages are bad and that everything's not roses all the time but why does she stay with him?'

'For the money, why else?' He'd opened his eyes and looked at her. 'My father made her sign a pre-nup and so if she signs the divorce papers, she gets nothing.'

'And so…what? They just argue and fight?'

'He's not violent. He'd never stoop to that but both of them have tempers. My mother likes to break the very expensive china plates.' He'd reached out a hand and brushed her hair behind her ear. 'Sometimes I think she does it purposely so she can go and buy a new set.'

'But what about you? Surely they're OK with you? Not being mean. Not to you.'

Fletch had leaned over and kissed her nose. 'I love so many things about you, Molly, and one of those is your occasional innocence.'

'Does that mean they *were* horrible to you, too?'

'Oh, everything is done with the utmost civility. It's not as though they throw things at me or smash china plates at my feet.'

'Then what did they do?'

'Ignored me when it suited them or lavished me with attention simply to annoy the other. Once, my father bought me a very expensive dirt bike just to annoy my mother as she wanted to spend money on recarpeting the house.'

'How old were you?'

He'd thought for a moment. 'I was home from boarding school so I must have been about eleven or twelve.'

'You went to boarding school?'

'It was better than stay at home with the two of them.'

Molly had kissed him firmly, slipping her arms about his neck and holding him close. 'Poor Fletch. Poor young Fletch, poor teenage Fletch, poor adult Fletch. I wish I could have saved you.'

He'd chuckled at her words and kissed her back. 'You've saved me now, Molly, and I can't thank you enough.'

She'd raised her eyebrows suggestively. 'Well... you could try.' She'd giggled as he'd responded by kissing her with more determination, caressing her with more tenderness, and making sweet love to his beautiful wife.

When Molly awoke the next morning, she could hear Fletcher next door, whistling as he moved about in the kitchen. Had he always liked cooking in the morning? She could remember him bringing her breakfast in bed on the odd occasion but that was usually when he was home for the short periods of time.

He'd ended up spending more time on the eastern coast of Australian than the western.

'But that's all in the past,' she whispered to herself as she climbed out of bed, stretching languorously before heading towards the bathroom. She smiled at her reflection.

'Such lovely dreams. Such lovely memories.' She sighed with delight, pleased that she did have good memories of their time together. Perhaps… if he weren't with Eliza…there might have been the slightest chance that they could…

She stopped the thought. Nothing would come of going down that path and right now she wanted to bask a bit longer in her wonderful dreams of the man who had stolen her heart so long ago and might…*might* still have it.

CHAPTER NINE

FLETCHER WALKED INTO his side of the duplex and threw his keys onto the table by the door. He looked at the wall, the wall that connected his place with Molly's. It had been a hectic day, lecturing and answering questions and doing his best to have minimal contact with the woman who was still legally his wife.

Tomorrow evening he would be alone with her in a car, driving to her siblings' house to spend the weekend with the only real family he'd ever known. Although it had only been for a short time and although it had been many years ago, Fletch still had a deep fondness and connection with his sisters-in-law. He'd also been deeply saddened to hear about the death of Arn and Letisha because Arn had certainly been more of a father to him than his own father.

It was one of the reasons why he wished he'd at least kept in loose contact with Molly because he would most definitely have dropped everything in order to attend their funeral, to be there to support Molly and the rest of the family. It was also his main reason for wanting to establish a level of friendship with Molly now. Yes, their lives were headed in different directions—she would soon be qualified and be wanting to flex her surgical experience and he would be…married…again. Married to Eliza.

As he headed into the kitchen to make himself a light dinner, he knew he had to call Eliza. He hadn't spoken to her since he'd arrived in Sydney. Well, he'd spoken to her voicemail, leaving several messages to let her know how things were going.

'She's clearly busy with her father,' he told himself as he sautéed onions and finished chopping the mushrooms. 'Hospital appointments, helping him recover from the treatment…' He stopped mumbling to himself as he heard the door next door open and close. Molly was home. Standing still, he listened, closing his eyes as he imagined her moving around next door, going up the hallway towards her bedroom or the kitchen. He waited and only moved when he realised the onions were starting to burn. He quickly opened his eyes and scolded himself for getting side-tracked once again by Molly. Molly who was still his wife.

When he heard the water start for her shower, he groaned with repressed frustration. Why were the walls between their places so thin? Since he'd moved in just a few short days ago—although it felt incredibly longer—he'd had trouble sleeping and so, when he was up and moving around at all hours of the night, he'd tried his best to keep his clattering and fumbling to a minimum so as not to wake her.

It wasn't normal for him not to sleep but being this close to Molly caused his mind to remain in 'active' mode for most of the evening. He would reflect on how they'd met, on how they'd become friends, on how they'd simply enjoyed spending time with each other. He remembered with perfect clarity the first time he'd kissed her and how she'd been incredibly concerned that it would wreck their new friendship. He remembered telling her that was impossible, that what he felt when he kissed her was nothing like he'd ever felt before.

'This is true love, Molly,' he'd whispered near her ear. 'This sort of love doesn't come around every day.'

And he still believed that. He'd loved Molly with all his heart but then…then he'd ruined everything. Yes, it had been a long time ago and, yes, he regretted every word he'd said to her when she'd told him about Katie. Ever since he'd arrived in Sydney, seeing her again and feeling that overwhelming attraction, that sense of true love, flowing through him, once more knocking him for six, Fletcher hadn't been able to stop playing the 'what if' game.

What if he weren't with Eliza? What if he and Molly followed through on the frightening natural chemistry that still existed between them? What if they decided to give it another go…to stay married?

He shook his head and returned his attention back to cooking his omelette. He was a fool to even contemplate that scenario because he knew, deep down inside, that Molly would never be able to forgive him for what he'd said to her. *He* couldn't even forgive himself so he really didn't expect her to.

'So that's that,' he told himself as he ignored the thought that Molly was on the other side of the wall, standing naked in the shower, beneath the spray of refreshing water.

He took his plate into the lounge room, further away from where she was, and switched on the television, needing to drown out the memories his mind was accessing. It was far too easy for him to imagine what she would look like because he knew all too well how her blonde hair became slightly darker when it was wet, how it would be slicked back from her face, how she would use a loofa to exfoliate her supple skin, the white frothy bubbles sliding down her perfect curves. Oh, yes, he had far too many memories of Molly in the shower, memories of him joining her, memories of them…together…wet and soapy and making slow, slippery love.

When his phone rang, startling him so completely that he was glad he'd put his full dinner plate onto the coffee table, he snatched it up more than pleased with the interruption.

'Dr Thompson,' he stated briskly before quickly clearing his throat, amazed at how husky his tone was.

'Fletcher?'

'Eliza!' Guilt instantly washed over him and he eased back into the chair, closing his eyes, wishing he'd at least checked the caller identification before answering. Not that he wouldn't have answered her call, but he might have composed himself a bit more before speaking to his fiancée, especially as he'd just been fantasising about another woman.

'How, er…' he cleared his throat again '…how are you? How's your dad?' He reached for the remote control and turned the television off so he could hear Eliza better.

'He's doing much better. I'm really proud of him. He's had his second course of chemotherapy and still hasn't been having too many side effects.'

'That *is* excellent news.'

'I'm so glad I was able to come and be with him, which reminds me, I think I might stay here for a while longer, if that's OK with you.'

'You don't need to ask my permission,' he stated. 'Of course you must stay with your father. He needs you, plus it will be a good break for you and you can catch up with all your old friends, spend some more time with your son and just relax.'

'That's what I thought. I didn't realise how much of a break I needed until I started to unwind a little. Your emails have been interesting. I'm sorry we kept missing each other's calls. How are things going there?'

'Good. Good.' He glanced at the wall, grimacing as he heard something like a chair clattering across the floor before Molly cried out in pain. He immediately stood with concern and took two steps towards the door before hearing her doing her 'stubbed toe' song. Fletch couldn't help but smile as he settled back down, knowing how she would be holding the sore foot in her hand, hopping around the place saying over and over, 'I've stubbed my toe, I've stubbed my toe, I've stubbed my toe.' At some point during his life with Molly, he'd seen both her sisters do the same dance in exactly the same way. When he'd asked her about it, she'd laughed.

'It was Letisha's idea when we were kids. She said that when you stub your toe, it hurts so much that if you hold your foot and hop around and sing the "I've stubbed my toe" song, then it helps to take your mind off the pain and, plus, it makes everyone else around you laugh, thereby releasing your own tension and frustration.'

'Huh' had been his answer. 'Letisha's a smart woman.'

'That she is, and she'll make an excellent mother to Jasmine and whatever other children she and my father have.' Then Molly had smiled at him and snuggled closer, sighing contentedly.

'Fletcher? Are you still there?' Eliza's voice came down the line.

He snapped his thoughts back to the present. 'Yes. Yes. Sorry, Eliza. What did you say?'

'I was asking how things were going at Sydney General. How many surgeries are you doing there?'

'At least four.'

'Four? Wow. You've had more patients agree to the surgery?'

'It's been incredible, Eliza. The more I can do, the more I can train others. I've done one and I'm doing the next one tomorrow, then two next week with a few of the consultant surgeons assisting.'

'Have you had Molly assist you yet?'

He nodded even though she couldn't see him.

'She was the one I did first…er…the first surgery, that is,' he quickly clarified his answer and Eliza chuckled.

'I knew what you meant. How is she?'

'Molly?'

'No, the Queen of Sheba,' she chided. 'Of course I meant Molly, you dope.' Eliza chuckled again. 'Sounds as though your mind is a bit scattered but I guess it's to be expected. Living next door to the woman you used to be married to while working with her at the hospital and also asking her to sign new divorce papers, as well as having your fiancée in Melbourne looking after her sick father—' Eliza stopped to take a breath. 'Yeah, you've got a lot going on in that brilliant mind of yours.'

Fletch couldn't help but smile. 'You're one of the most understanding women I've ever met.'

'That's because we've been upfront with each other,' Eliza stated. 'Loneliness didn't suit either of us and there are worse reasons to pursue a marriage rather than wanting a companion and close friend for the next twenty or so years.'

'This is very true.' He had been lonely before he'd met Eliza. He'd been living just for his work, for his patients, and he'd been doing that for far too long. Initially when he and Molly had separated, he'd enjoyed throwing himself into his work, but after such a long time it was Eliza who had made him realise that always giving to others would only end with him getting burnt out. After that, she'd invited him out for coffee and the basis for their non-working friendship had been established.

They'd often gone out as friends, seeing a movie, enjoying a theatre production, going to farmers' markets. This was the type of life Fletcher hadn't been used to, as living and working overseas in Third World countries didn't often leave time for such luxuries. Then, once the tour had actually begun and he'd been working and travelling every few weeks, Eliza his only constant companion, their friendship had increased, blossoming into a genuine fondness for each other.

When she had proposed to him, not only had he been surprised but she'd been insistent that he understand that her first husband, Scotty, would always be the true love of her life.

'Before he died, he implored me not to be alone

for the rest of my life and at the time I didn't listen because I had my son with me, but now he's off at medical school, finding his own life—just as he should be.'

'And you're left on your own.'

'And lonely.' She'd grasped his hand and shaken her head. 'I don't want to be lonely any more, Fletcher. I don't think you do, either.'

So Fletcher had thought about what she'd said, about how his previous marriage to Molly had been based solely on love and that marriage had ended in heartbreak. Perhaps a 'marriage of convenience', where he was incredibly fond of his wife, would be better, would be less painful. Yet when he'd discovered his marriage to Molly was still legally binding, he'd felt as though he'd been offered a second chance. Still, he was a man of his word and, as such, he would honour his commitment to Eliza.

'Fletcher,' Eliza said down the line, 'my dad's calling for me, so I'd better go. Call me on the weekend and we'll have a good catch up then.'

'Uh…actually, I'm going away for the weekend.' He raked a hand through his hair as he contemplated telling Eliza of his plans. 'Molly needs to get the document she was sent from the law-yers so I can give it to my cousin and the letter is in Newcastle at her sister's house.'

'Oh, OK. So you're headed to Newcastle?'

Fletch frowned at the complete understanding in her tone. 'Er...yeah.'

'That'll be great. You can catch up with her family again.'

'Yes.' He frowned. 'Eliza, aren't you even the least bit concerned? I mean, I'm going with Molly to her family's home for the weekend. Most fian-cées would be a bit...you know...jealous.'

Her soft laughter tinkled down the phone line. 'I'm just not the jealous type, Fletcher, and be-sides, I trust you. Have a good time and call me when you can.'

'OK.'

'Love you. Bye.' Her words were quickly fol-lowed by a muffled, 'Coming, Dad.'

'Bye, Eliza,' he murmured to the disconnected line. Fletch put the phone back onto the table be-fore sitting down to eat his now cold dinner. Why was it that after that phone call to Eliza, the first time he'd spoken to her and not her voicemail or emailed her since he'd arrived in Sydney, he was left feeling flat? It was right that she trusted him so completely, wasn't it? It showed great strength of character, what an incredible woman Eliza was.

After finishing his cold meal, he made himself a cup of herbal tea then, as he could hear the quiet din of Molly's television from next door, he headed outside onto the front porch. The night was cool but not cold and the moon was almost cut directly in half. The stars didn't appear too bright given that he was staying near the middle of the city. Crossing his arms, he sauntered out onto the front path and gazed up at the sky. The brightest light was an aeroplane, coming in to land, flying so low it looked as if it were about to land on the major road nearby.

'They've only just recently changed the flight path for some of the planes,' Molly said softly behind him, and he turned to see her standing in her doorway, haloed with light from behind. His gut immediately tightened and he wanted nothing more than to cross to her side, haul her into his arms and press his mouth to hers. He forced himself to turn away and gaze up at the sky once more, needing to ignore the way she made him feel while at the same time telling himself that everything he felt towards her was just a residual memory. Nothing more.

'I'm still getting used to it,' she remarked and this time her words were a little louder as he heard the soft click of the door as she pulled it closed behind her. She came to stand beside him, arms crossed, head back, looking up at the sky.

Neither of them spoke for quite a while, both content to allow the night and all its city sounds to envelop them. 'It's nice here,' he eventually said.

'I do prefer Newcastle but here's not so bad.'

'Do you think you'll return there once you're qualified?' He didn't look at her as he spoke but he didn't need to, both of them still staring up at the sky.

'For a while, perhaps, until I can figure out what it is I want to do with my new-found qualifications. Who knows, I may end up working for Pacific Medical Aid.'

'Is that so?' He couldn't help but smile. 'Does this have anything to do with my influence?'

Molly chuckled softly, the sound deeper and richer than Eliza's. He gave his thoughts a mental shake to stop himself from comparing them.

'Or it might have something to do with the fact that my brother-in-law works closely in Tarparnii with PMA and my nephew *is* Tarparnese.'

Fletch considered her words for a moment. 'Or that,' he added, looking down at her with a small grin on his face. 'It's good, though, that you're thinking of heading over there. Or, for that matter, anywhere that needs good medical services. There are other countries PMA work in apart from Tarparnii and there are other organisations who work in Africa and Bangladesh and—'

'Hold on there, bud,' she interrupted with another soft laugh, the sound washing over him, making him feel relaxed and calm. Fletch hadn't even realised he'd been tensing his muscles until now. Being around Molly, nice and calm like this, the two of them just talking softly, had always managed to release his tension. 'You don't need to sell me on this concept. Cora did that a long time ago.'

'Ah…sibling peer pressure. There's no competing with that, at least as far as I know.'

Molly acknowledged his words but took a moment to reply. 'Was it very lonely, growing up with no siblings?'

'You've asked me that question before,' he replied.

'Really? What was your answer?'

'Clearly one that didn't stick in your memory,' he mused.

'Well?' she prompted impatiently when he didn't immediately continue. Fletcher laughed. 'I'm so pleased you still find my impatience so amusing.'

'Oh. She remembers *that*. And it wasn't just your impatience I found amusing, Molly, it was your gung-ho-ness. You were always willing to take on a challenge and if anyone doubted you, boy, would you figuratively push up your sleeves and storm into the fray with an "I'll show them" attitude.'

'I am who I am. The last of three, and you still haven't told me what it was like growing up with no siblings.'

Fletcher sighed and shoved his hands into his pockets. 'It was…'

'Lonely?'

'No. I was always surrounded by servants or nannies. I was home schooled until I was eleven years old and then I went to boarding school.'

'I remember that part. Was it quiet?'

'Never quiet.' He rolled his eyes. 'Not with my parents around yelling and smashing things.' He was startled when Molly put her hand onto his arm. He looked down at her, not surprised to see that caring gleam in her eyes. Although it was dark, although the moon wasn't providing them with much light, he didn't need to have illumination to know the expressions on her face. He knew them by heart. Had experienced each and every one of them during their time together and, right now, he knew her empathy for him was uppermost in her thoughts.

'I do remember now. I remember you telling me it was…nothingness. You didn't know any different.'

'Not until I went to boarding school and, believe me, I had trouble adjusting to being surrounded by so many people I found it difficult to have any solitude.'

'Do you still want solitude?' Her words were quiet yet the question seemed to be extremely loud. Was she asking him something else? Asking him if he was lonely now? He uncrossed his arms and patted her hand before shifting away from her.

'Fletch? What's wrong?'

'What makes you think anything's wrong?' Even as he said the words he knew what her reaction was going to be.

'Are you serious? You're asking *me* that question? I know you better than the back of my hand.'

'OK, then. Tell me what's wrong?' He took a few steps back towards the porch, needing a bit of distance from her. It was strange being back with her, having these sorts of discussions.

'Well, for a start, you're acting defensive. What's got into you?'

Fletch looked down at the ground, realising what she was saying was the truth.

'I mean one minute we're joking together and the next, you're all Mr Prickly.'

'I know, I know. You're right.' He nodded. 'I guess it's just a little…odd, being with someone who knows you so well after all this time.'

'What about Eliza? Doesn't she know you well?'

He angled his head to the side and pondered

her words for a moment. 'I guess we're still getting to know each other.'

'How long have you been working together?'

'About eighteen months.'

'Is that how long you've been a…couple?' Had he imagined it or did her voice change as she said the last word.

He shook his head. 'Less than that. We were good friends for a long time. I guess it's probably a bit quick, really.'

'You think that's quick?' Molly chuckled. 'Fletch, we were married before we'd known each other for *one* month.'

'What are you trying to get at, Molly?' He frowned.

'I'm not trying to get at anything, Fletch, other than sometimes some people just click. It was what you said to me all those years ago when we were travelling. You and I, we just clicked. And sometimes, people take a little longer to get to know each other. Like you and your Eliza.'

'And you and *your* Roger?' he couldn't help pointing out. The problem was, he knew exactly what Molly was talking about. The two of them had been joined together in thought, in humour and, later, in body. She was the only woman he'd connected with on that level. If such a thing as soulmates existed then he'd have to confess that he was standing opposite his now, arguing with her.

She looked amazing when she was like this. Hands on hips. Chin lifted with defiance. She was right. He didn't know Eliza as well as he knew her but what he shared with Eliza was more akin to companionship, a mutual respect. Yet watching Molly as she started giving him a piece of her mind, her fiery temper starting to show, he couldn't help but smile.

'And stop smiling!' She even stamped her foot in anger and the smile turned into a chuckle. 'I mean it, Fletcher.'

'I know you do.' He paused then, held up his index finger towards her. 'Sorry. Can you just go back a bit? Did I hear you say you'd ended things with Roger?' He'd been so busy admiring her vivacity that he hadn't really been focusing on her words.

'We were always more friends than anything else.'

He was amazed at how both of them seemed to

have sought other relationships that were more based upon friendship rather than anything else.

'There you go again, smiling at me for no reason. And…hang on.' She shook her finger at him. 'I was mad with you. Stop changing the subject, making me forget.' She sighed heavily. 'I used to hate it when you did that and I still do.'

'That's because I'm the only person in the world with such skills.' He blew on his fingers and brushed them on his lapel. 'Apart from your sisters, of course.'

Molly slowly shook her head, clearly bemused by the way they could just chat and argue and debate. 'Funny how we've slipped back into our old habits, eh? One minute we're stargazing, the next we're arguing and then we're all smiles.' The question was rhetorical and he chuckled, knowing she didn't really need an answer.

She was right, though. They'd fallen easily back into their old habits but some habits hadn't been good ones. Those, they needed to avoid at all costs.

'Oh, by the way, are you all set for surgery with Alexis tomorrow? She's so nervous.'

'I've had several meetings with her and sorted everything out.'

'Good.' Molly nodded, then paused as though she was going to say something else but then stopped. She scratched the back of her head, then looked up at him. 'Does…your Eliza know you're coming to Newcastle with me?' Her tone was soft as well as concerned.

'Yes.'

'And she's OK with that? I mean, with you spending the weekend with your ex-in-laws and me?'

'Technically, they're not "ex".'

'You know what I mean, Fletch. Is Eliza really OK with everything?'

'She told me to have a good time catching up and reminiscing.'

Molly raised her eyebrows in surprise. 'Huh.'

'What?'

'Nothing.'

'Tell me. You know I hate it when you do that.'

'I was just thinking that you have a very understanding partner, that's all.'

'She is understanding,' he confirmed.

'She's a better person than me. I mean, I'd be as jealous as anything.'

'You would?'

'Oh, yes. I was always jealous when you would flirt with the pretty nurses.'

'I never flirted with them. Not while we were married.'

'Technically you know that's not true given we're still married,' she pointed out.

'I didn't realise you were such a pedant, Molly,' he added, still sort of pleased that she'd been jealous back then. 'You never had any cause to be jealous, Molly. You know that, right?' Fletcher met her gaze. 'It was always you. Always.'

His words were soft and intent. The tension around them started to increase and he took a step forward, wanting to tell her he was so incredibly sorry, to apologise again and again for being such a jerk and to beg for her forgiveness.

'I'd better head inside.' Molly pointed to her door. It was dangerous, being out here with Fletcher, hearing him say that it had always been her and no one else. Now, though, that was completely untrue. It *wasn't* her and there *was* someone else.

'Goodnight, Fletcher,' she said, putting her hand on the door handle and offering him one last smile before going inside. She might not have had cause to be jealous in the past but she was certainly jealous now.

CHAPTER TEN

'WHAT HAS GOT into you?' Alexis asked her as they changed out of their theatre garb. Alexis had been in theatre with Fletcher that afternoon, having her turn at learning the techniques of the device he'd invented. Everything had gone to plan and Alexis was on a high.

'Nothing.' Molly had just finished the afternoon theatre surgical list and was busy changing.

'No. Something's wrong. I can sense it.'

'It's only because you're on such a high, everyone else seems rather dull in comparison. Besides, surgery and study do have a way of sucking the life out of a person but I just keep reassuring myself that it's almost over. Exams are looming—'

'Don't remind me.'

'And then we'll be qualified surgeons,' she continued, ignoring Alexis's interruption.

'And do you think the stress is going to get any

less after that? Then we have to find jobs by either getting employed by the hospital or opening our own private practice or—'

'Or going overseas and doing some work in countries that really need good surgeons.'

Alexis's eyebrows hit her hairline. 'You're serious about that?'

'I thought you were, too.' Molly brushed out her curls into smooth waves, then put her brush back into her locker. 'Working for an agency such as Pacific Medical Aid looks fantastic on the résumé and also assists with procuring future employment.'

Alexis shook her head, her smile increasing. 'Or is it that your smashing ex-husband has been chewing your ear…figuratively and literally?'

Molly leaned against her locker and closed her eyes. 'He's getting married again, Alexis.'

'What?'

Molly opened her eyes and pushed away from the lockers, hooking her bag over her shoulder. She dragged in a deep breath, trying to control the rising sense of dejection she'd been experiencing ever since she'd realised why he'd wanted the divorce.

'Molly? What is it?'

'Nothing. I'm just tired.'

Alexis was instantly by her side. She put her hands on Molly's shoulders. 'What is it?'

Molly looked at her friend and was surprised when tears immediately sprang to her eyes. 'It's more difficult to control your emotions when people are being nice to you,' she commented with a sniff.

'So don't control them. Talk to me.'

'I'm…um…apparently…' She cleared her throat. 'I'm still married to Fletcher.'

'What?' Alexis stared at Molly in disbelief. 'I thought you said you *were* married to him.'

'The only reason he's needed to spend time with me—apart from the whole invention thing with his surgical device—is so he can get the piece of paper I received from the lawyers all those years ago which proves we're not divorced.'

'What?' This time, Alexis's tone was filled with confusion and puzzlement. 'That makes no sense. How can you not be divorced?'

Molly shook her head and sighed as she reached into her pocket for a tissue. Alexis dropped her hands but continued staring at her friend. 'It's too hard to explain but the point is, he only needs the piece of paper so we can refile for the divorce so that he can marry this other woman—Eliza. Who, by the way, sounds really nice and completely understanding. She doesn't even seem to care that Fletcher and I are going away together for the weekend.'

'What?' Alexis's eyes were wide open with stunned amazement. 'You're spending the weekend with him?'

'At home. In Newcastle. That's where the document is that he needs.'

'So why does he need to go with you?'

Molly shrugged. 'He wants to see Cora and Stacey again. We were all a family once.'

Alexis frowned. 'I guess. And his fiancée doesn't care?'

'She's fine with it, apparently.'

'I wouldn't be.'

'Neither would I. I guess she's not the jealous type.' Molly blew her nose, feeling better for having blurted out her thoughts and emotions to her friend. 'At least I'll have my family around to cocoon and coddle me.'

Alexis gave Molly a big hug. 'When do you leave?'

'Soon. I just need to go home and finish throwing some things into a bag.'

'OK, then. Travel safe.'

'And you go out and celebrate.' Molly pointed sternly to her friend. 'You did an excellent job with that surgery. You deserve to reward yourself.'

'You've got that right!' Alexis's earlier smile returned and the two of them walked out of the changing rooms together. It was only as they reached the theatre clerk's desk near the doors that Molly realised Fletcher was standing there, clearly waiting for her because when he saw her he stopped talking to the clerk and gave her his full attention, smiling warmly.

'There you are. I was beginning to think you'd snuck out another door.'

'Nope. Ready to go?'

'Oh?' The theatre clerk grinned at them both suggestively. 'Where are the two of you going?'

'Out for a drink to celebrate the successful surgeries we've done,' Alexis commented quickly.

'You're welcome to join us at the pub across the road when you're done.'

The theatre clerk gave Fletcher a quick perusal and a feline smile. 'I might just do that.'

'And Fetching Fletcher strikes again,' Alexis said once they were clear of the theatre department.

Fletcher merely shrugged one shoulder. 'I simply cannot help it if I am found utterly irresistible by the opposite sex,' he joked.

'Ha.' Molly couldn't help but laugh, pleased he was at least in a good mood for the start of their weekend together.

'And not just the opposite sex, either,' Alexis said, winking at him before laughing. They went down the stairs and out into the early evening. 'What time are the two of you leaving?' she asked and Molly noticed Fletcher raise his eyebrows in surprise. 'Or do you actually have time for a quick celebratory drink across the road?' She jerked her thumb towards the pub.

'I think we can definitely squeeze in a non-alcoholic drink before we leave,' Fletcher remarked. 'Molly?'

'Absolutely.'

'A job well done for all of us,' Alexis said as they walked towards the pedestrian crossing.

'Well, not for Fletch,' Molly added. 'I'm sure by now he can do the surgery in his sleep.'

'Hmm. I did wonder why there were so many scalpel holes in my pillows.'

Alexis and Molly laughed and she felt the weight of her earlier oppression lift from her shoulders. What did it matter what Fletcher's plans were for the future? His life was his life just as her life was hers. She had plans to travel and help others and to be the best surgeon she could be. Why couldn't he have plans to marry someone else?

Determined to be happy for him, just as a true friend would be, she resolved to let go of her neuroses, at least for the weekend, so she could enjoy herself with her family.

After they'd had a drink with Alexis, they headed back to the duplex where they quickly finished packing, starting on the road only an hour later than originally planned.

'Nice hire car. Smooth.' She changed gears as she navigated her way through the end of the

Sydney evening rush-hour traffic. She was also glad he'd offered her the keys.

'Want to drive? I put your name on the hire contract.'

'You remembered how I like driving?'

'I did.'

As she manoeuvred the car out onto the motorway they discussed the surgery he'd performed with Alexis, as well as talking about the surgical cases she'd done in Theatre.

'It's so great to be able to talk about my day with you,' she said, soft jazz music playing in the background. 'You know the people I work with, you know their temperaments and personalities. It's nice.'

'Surely you can talk to your sisters about the cases?'

'Of course, but they don't know a lot of the actual people I work with, apart from Alexis. It just makes a difference when I say things like… David was underfoot again.'

'Ah. Yes. David. He's a jittery sort of fellow, isn't he?' He nodded. 'I know this is his first year on the surgical training programme but if he doesn't get rid of his nerves, he'll never make a good surgeon.'

'Surgeons need to have nerves of steel,' she said in a deep voice and they both laughed.

'Now, before we get to your house, tell me more about your siblings—the ones I don't know.'

Molly was more than happy to tell him about Jasmine's desire to go into medicine when she'd finished her schooling and how George and Lydia loved their rabbits. 'And along with Pierce's sister, Nell, they like entering their rabbits in the rabbit-jumping contests.'

'Rabbit-jumping contests?' He glanced at her in disbelief. 'You're pulling my leg.'

'Not at all. It's a very serious business and George, Lydia and Nell are devoted to it.'

'Then I shall listen intently to all they have to say on the subject.'

She smiled across at him. 'Thank you. That means a lot. Most men, when they discover I share guardianship of my younger siblings, tend to shy away from wanting anything to do with them.'

'I think you'll find, my dear Molly, that I am nothing like "most men".'

'True. You've always been the type of man to walk to the beat of your own drum.'

'I'm so glad you've noticed.'

'Oh, I noticed quite a long time ago, Fletch.' She glanced across at him as she slowed the car down to stop at traffic lights.

His voice dropped to an intimate whisper. 'There are quite a few things I've noticed about you, too.'

'Such as?' She knew she was fishing but couldn't help it.

'Such as you're more focused. You're still just as stubborn as you always were but now your stubbornness is more clearly directed.'

'Ha! You cheeky sod.' She laughed, enjoying spending time with him, just as she had in the past. This was how they'd been when they'd been travelling all those years ago, joking and teasing each other, laughing and enjoying themselves. It was nice to be able to do that again.

By the time she pulled the car into the driveway of her family home, she was more than ready to escape the confines of the enclosed capsule of the car.

'And about time you arrived,' Cora called as she

came out, her arms wide open towards Fletcher. 'It's really good to see you again,' she told him, enveloping him in a hug as though no time had passed at all. 'Brother-in-law.' She winked and before he could say anything, the rest of the clan trooped out to greet them.

The Wilton clan was even more rowdy than all those years ago, the family home filled with lots of love and laughter, and Fletcher couldn't remember the last time he'd felt so relaxed. Travelling, getting to know Eliza, seeing Molly again, had exhausted him far more than he'd realised, but learning about rabbit jumping, doing jigsaw puzzles and generally connecting again with Molly's family made him feel as though he'd never left.

It also made him realise just how much he'd missed having a real family. He hadn't even had the chance to meet Eliza's father yet but her son had joined them for a few weeks travelling around with them on mid-semester break. It had been good to get to know him but Eliza's family still didn't make him feel anything like he'd felt with the Wiltons. Being with the Wiltons all those years ago had helped him to realise what a family was supposed to be like because, until then, the only model he'd ever really known was his own dysfunctional one.

The laughter, the sharing, the helping. Even Pierce and Archer seemed so natural, so at home within this crazy family. Reading stories, making snacks, picking up toys, organising bath time, preparing meals, hanging out washing. There was always something to do and always someone to do it with and, although the large house could accommodate them all, it was difficult to walk down the hallway without meeting someone.

'I hadn't really realised how…isolated I've become,' he said to Eliza on Saturday evening when he called her. The day had been a full but fun one and he was lying on his single bed with one hand behind his head, the other holding his cell phone to his ear.

'Ouch. Thanks a lot,' Eliza replied with a laugh.

'That's not what I meant.' He spoke quickly, closing his eyes and cringing a little at his lack of decorum. 'Of course I have you but…well, you also have your father and your son.'

'I know what you're saying,' Eliza continued. 'Seeing Molly's family up close, remembering how you used to be a part of it…well, it's bound to bring back memories as well as the sense that something is missing from your own life.'

A picture of Molly instantly came to mind and his eyes snapped open in shock. Molly? Was Molly what was missing from his life? Molly and the possibility of a family of their own? No. No. He was with Eliza. He couldn't go back to where he and Molly had started. Could he?

It wouldn't be the same beginning, it would be a different beginning. They were different people after all, people with almost two decades' worth of different memories and more experience when it came to making relationships work.

'Fletcher?'

He brought his thoughts back to the present. 'Sorry, Eliza. I guess I'm a little preoccupied this evening.'

'Tonight's not the only night.' There was a softness to her words. 'I guess we've both been a little preoccupied lately.'

They'd already discussed her father's improving health and also how her son was progressing at medical school. 'You have a point.'

'Do you think, now that we're not travelling

together, that things seem a little…I don't know…' She searched for the right word.

'Forced between us?' He shook his head as he realised what he needed to do. Eliza made a good point and he couldn't promise that even once the fellowship ended, things wouldn't still seem forced or uncomfortable between them.

'Yes,' she agreed. 'Don't get me wrong, Fletcher, I love talking to you and hearing about what's happening in your life but…I don't spend all day long thinking about you, either. I guess it's because I'm so busy. Looking after a parent isn't easy but having my sisters dropping in and helping out, so that I can take some time to go and have lunch with my son, definitely helps.'

'While my focus has been on finishing the fellowship and trying to get this divorce thing sorted out.' Even as he said the words he felt a pang of regret, of sadness at the thought that one day soon, in a few months' time, he would be officially divorced from Molly. He'd had to go through the pain of losing her once, of assuming his divorce had been finalised, but then to discover they were still legally joined in holy matrimony had given him a small glimpse of an alternative future, one he'd never thought possible.

'Oh, Fletcher,' Eliza said after a moment's pause. 'Are we kidding ourselves?'

'What do you mean?'

'Perhaps it was a mistake—me proposing to you and you accepting.' She sighed. 'Why *did* you accept?'

'Because I thought we'd be able to make each other happy for the next twenty or thirty years.'

'But that was before you realised you were still legally married to Molly.'

'Well…yes.' He frowned. 'What are you saying?'

'I'm saying that I think we need to call off our engagement. I'm very fond of you and I would have been honoured to spend the rest of my life with you. You make me laugh, you've helped me not to take myself so seriously. You brought me out of the void I was in after my husband's death, out of that fog, and I can never thank you enough for that. Scotty was the love of my life, the father of my child, my soulmate and I can never see him again.' She paused. 'You, on the

other hand, you have actually been given a second chance to be with your soulmate.'

'Soulmate?' He raised his eyebrows and was
pleased when he heard her chuckle.

'Come on, Fletcher. It's not that difficult to
work it out. Who's the one woman you want to
see every day, who makes your heart race with
excitement, who drives you completely insane,
who is the first person you want to tell your good
and bad news?'

'Molly.' He breathed her name.

'Exactly. I can tell by the way you talk about
her, by the way you try and disguise what you're
really feeling by making your accounts more
professional. You also seem to go silent on the
phone, no doubt drifting off into some old memory of the two of you together.' She sighed and
Fletcher listened intently, trying not to feel terrible that their time together was coming to an end.
'I know these things, Fletcher, because I've been
there. I've lived off my old memories for so long
and I'll continue to do so but I've realised—*you
have helped me to realise*—that it's OK to visit
those memories but to take delight in the people

around me. My son, especially, as well as my father and sisters.'

'Eliza, I—'

'Fletcher, it's quite clear to me that your feelings for Molly are still very much alive. I would never want to stand in the way of that sort of love. Take it while you can. Hold on to it for as long as you can. Life is short, far too short to have regrets. This is the right thing to do, Fletcher. For both of us.'

'And we'll stay friends? I don't want to lose you as a friend.'

'No chance of that,' Eliza told him with a chuckle. 'When you're all done with the fellowship—and you've managed to sort things out with Molly—come to Melbourne. I'd love to meet her. She sounds like such a wonderful person.'

'She is.' He smiled, feeling as though an enormous weight had just been lifted from his shoulders, from his head, from his heart. No more conflicting emotions. No feeling guilty. No more hiding from the way he really felt about Molly. He concluded his call to Eliza—his ex-fiancée—and started making plans on how best to convince his legal wife to remain his legal wife, for ever.

'Molly.' He breathed her name and smiled, his heart singing with love for her.

CHAPTER ELEVEN

'HOW ARE YOU holding up?' she asked him on Sunday morning at breakfast. She was brighter, happier and completely content. He could remember it always being that way when she was with her family. The three of them, Stacey, Cora and Molly, were such an integral part of each other, sharing a bond that no one else could really understand, but it certainly made them all happy and he loved seeing her that way. Her hair was less curly here, bouncing around her shoulders in soft waves, enticing him to touch. Her green eyes were vibrant, compelling him to stare into them all day long. Her smile was wide and bright and perfect, making him want to kiss her lips and never stop.

There was no denying his attraction to her. Not any more. After his conversation with Eliza last night, he was a free man. Free to pursue Molly. Free to woo her. Free to convince her that staying married to him was the right…was the *only* decision.

Being here with her family, getting to know Jasmine, George and Lydia as well as Stacey's husband, Pierce, and his sister, Nell, reacquainting himself with Cora's husband, Archer, and meeting their adopted son, Ty, only confirmed that this was what he wanted, this was the place where he felt more at home than any other place in the world. He'd lived overseas, travelled and worked in too many countries to count but never had he gained a pure sense of family, of belonging, as he did right here, right now, sitting at the dining-room table with Molly, staring at her with such an intensity that he was positive she started to blush.

'Are you going to answer my question or are you just going to sit there and stare at me?'

'Definitely the latter,' he commented. That was another thing his time here in Newcastle had confirmed. He loved Molly. He was completely and utterly in love with Molly Wilton. He wanted to have children with her, to find a job in Australia, preferably in Sydney or Newcastle so she could be close to her siblings.

Their children would have her blonde curls and his blue eyes. They would spend time with their aunties and uncles, play with their cousins. They would be raised in a completely different environment from that he'd had to suffer through. They would be loved, not only by their parents, but by their extended family. They would be made to feel their worth, to grow to be secure and happy adults.

He and Molly could do this. They could be a family together, the family they'd planned to be all those years ago. That dream could become a reality for both of them and the thought of that prospect made him sigh with contentment. It felt right. It felt as though this was where he'd meant to be his whole life and, although he'd regretted his past actions, he was being handed a second chance. Hope soared within him. Was this much happiness possible again? He had to at least try.

'Fletch.' She smiled as she spoke his name softly, her gaze brightening with delight at his answer. 'You're still staring at me.'

'I know. I'm enjoying it.' He reached out and took her hand in his, raising it to his lips and brushing a soft kiss across her knuckles.

'Fletcher?' She tried to remove her hand but he only linked his fingers with hers. 'What about Eliza?' Her voice was a whisper and she glanced around lest any of her family should see them.

'I spoke to Eliza last night.' He shook his head slowly, not taking his gaze from hers. 'And… well…long story short—we're not together any more.'

'What?' The word was barely audible, her eyes widening with surprise. Was it a delighted surprise? Was it a shocked surprise? Was it a repulsed surprise? 'You called off your engagement?'

'Yes…er…well, she did actually but it was a mutual decision. We're still going to remain friends.' Fletch smiled and kissed her hand once again.

'But Eliza's OK with it? Isn't it a bit sudden to just end it like that? On the phone? Don't you at least want to see her and—'

He reached out and put a finger gently across her lips to stop her talking. What he'd really wanted to do was to keep her quiet by pressing his mouth to hers but he felt that might have been jumping the gun a little bit. It was true that the attraction between them was still very much alive but that didn't mean that she would be willing to try again.

'Shh. It's all fine.' He lowered his hand to stop himself from touching her further. Slowly, slowly. 'Eliza and I were never really in love with each other.'

'You…you weren't?' The words hitched in her throat, as though she was completely out of breath. 'But you were going to get married!'

'Neither of us wanted to be lonely for the rest of our lives. Our relationship was formed out of a deep fondness for each other but…very recently,' he murmured, brushing another small kiss to her hand, 'I've come to realise that I want more than just a deep fondness.'

'Really?'

'Oh, yes.' He stared at her again, his words pointed as his gaze flicked to encompass her lips before he met her eyes again.

She swallowed, her lips parting slightly, enticing him to taste them. Didn't she have any idea just how crazy he was for her? She closed her eyes for a brief second, as though she was having trouble thinking. 'You were…uh…lonely?'

Her fingers tightened on his, letting him know that she cared about his feelings.

He smiled sadly and nodded. 'I don't have a plethora of siblings to share my life with. I don't even have parents who are interested in me. They live in Spain and I live...' He paused, not even sure where he did live. 'I live wherever I find myself. For years, I threw myself into my work. First I did it to try and forget.'

'Forget?'

'About you. About Katie. About that whole part of my life.'

'You wanted to forget me?'

He nodded. 'I was hurt. I was angry, not with you but with myself for being such a jerk.'

'And now?'

'Now, I've had a lot of time to put things into some sort of perspective. Travelling and helping people really was a balm for my soul and I learned so much. For a long time, that was enough, it was all I needed. Then, when I was offered the fellowship, it seemed to be the right thing to do. Not only did it give me the opportunity to publicise my device and to teach other surgeons the correct way of using it, but it gave me the chance to spend a good portion of my time back home. I love Australia. I've missed it far more than I realised.'

'It's a good place to live. So you're not planning to travel any more? Is that what you're saying?'

Was that hope he'd heard in her tone? He watched her expression closely as he continued. 'I guess what I'm trying to say is that travelling the world, not having a definitive place to call home, no…family…to come back to, isn't what I'm after any more.'

'Family?' Molly edged back a little at his words, loosening her grip on his hand. 'You want to have children?' She stared at him for a bit longer, clearly trying to read his expression. He knew he couldn't hide the truth, not with the way he'd been staring at her, kissing her hand, talking about a future and a family. 'You want to have children *with me*?' She squeaked the last two words.

'Molly…' He stopped, looking into her eyes, and when she slowly shook her head from side to side he wished she weren't so adept at reading his expressions.

'You think that you and I can just pick up

where we left off and become a family again?'
Her tone was filled with incredulity and in another moment she disengaged her hand from his
and pushed back her chair, standing to stare at
him as though he'd just grown an extra head.
'Fletch—I—'

She stopped, opening and closing her mouth a
few times.

'You look like a goldfish.'

'I'm…I'm stunned.' She shook her head and
walked into the kitchen, switching on the coffee
machine. Thankfully, the house was quiet, Pierce
and Stacey having taken the kids out to church
and the others were sleeping, but soon everyone
would be home and awake and the noise would
start again. She closed her eyes for a second,
wishing Fletcher hadn't said anything.

Memories from the past blended with memories of the present, blurring the lines. She liked
being with Fletcher and she had to admit that
he'd fitted seamlessly back into her family. Her
sisters had welcomed him as though he really
was a long-lost family member. He seemed to
get along very well with Archer and Pierce and
he had endless patience with Lydia and George.

Even Jasmine, who was highly protective of the family, had been laughing with him last night, bonding over a movie they'd both seen.

How did she feel about him? *Really* feel about him? She'd done her best to keep that door firmly closed, especially as he'd been engaged to another woman, but now...now that was over. He was essentially a free man. Well, apart from still being legally married to her.

She was legally married to him!

Her heart started pounding faster and her mouth went dry as she realised the truth of their situation. With the way Fletcher was talking, it was as though he didn't really want to sign the divorce papers. How did she feel about that? About remaining married to—

She stopped her thoughts and tried to concentrate on making the coffee. Grinding the coffee. Tamping it down. Hooking it into position. All the while her thoughts were jumbling over each other. All the while she was conscious of the fact that she could feel Fletcher's gaze watching her every move. How did she feel about Fletcher? How *did* she feel about Fletcher? Well, of course she loved him. She would always love him but was that love the love of a brother? A close friend? A husband? A passionate lover?

She tried to ignore the fervent pounding of her heart as her mind realised that the thrilling dreams she'd had about him, the ones where he kissed every inch of her body and made her wild with aching desire, could actually come true.

Molly closed her eyes, breathing out slowly, her imagination taking flight.

'Molly?' His sexy deep voice cut across her thoughts and she immediately opened her eyes, reaching out towards the coffee machine and turning on the steam wand by accident, the hot air hissing out over her other hand.

'Ouch!' She shut it off and quickly turned and stalked to the sink, put her hand under running cold water. 'Stupid. Stupid. Stupid.' Her words were a harsh whisper as she chided herself.

'Let me see.'

She jumped, not realising he'd come to stand beside her.

'It's fine.' She tried to jerk her hand away but he wasn't having any of it.

'Let. Me. See.' His tone brooked no argument

and he took her hand in his. 'You're so stubborn sometimes.'

'Yes. Yes, I am. You should know that.'

He scrutinised her hand before bringing it to his lips to kiss it before putting it back beneath the cold running water. 'You'll be fine.'

'I know. I am a doctor, too.'

Fletcher only chuckled at her outburst and calmly finished making them both a coffee.

'It isn't funny, Fletcher. Any of this.' Molly turned off the tap and carefully dried her hand before finding the moisturiser and rubbing some in.

'Understood,' he remarked, handing her a cup of coffee. 'Why don't we sit outside and talk about things?'

'I don't want to talk, Fletcher.'

'Oh?' He raised his eyebrows teasingly. 'You want to…cuddle instead?'

'Cuddle?' Molly glared at him for a long moment before taking the cup from him and walking outside into the cool September morning. She knew Fletcher would follow her, that they would talk even though she didn't really want to. It was all too confusing, too heart-wrenching. She knew she was opening the door to her heart wider and wider the more time they spent together.

She'd brought him home to her family! Why had she done that? Seeing him blend in so seamlessly with them all, laughing with him, relaxing with him…it had been like old times. Sipping her coffee, she walked over the slightly dewy grass towards the rabbit cages. The animals were huddling together, their little noses twitching, both of them quite content. 'What's your secret?' She crouched down and made kissing noises to them. 'Am I making a fool of myself?'

'You're asking rabbits for advice.' The deep answer came from behind her and she quickly stood and turned to face Fletcher, almost spilling her coffee.

'I didn't hear you.'

'What's wrong, Molly?'

'What makes you think there's—'

'I know you,' he interrupted, taking her cup from her and setting it down next to his on a nearby stone flower box. 'Come on. What is it?'

Molly threw her arms in the air and exhaled loudly with exasperation. 'Everything!' She stalked away from the cage. 'I hate not knowing what's going on and now with you...I'm so confused, Fletcher.'

'What is there to be confused about?'

'How can you be so calm? I saw that look on your face, the one that said you and I should give it another try.'

He glanced down at his shoes before meeting her gaze once more. 'True.'

'Did you break things off with Eliza because of me?'

'Yes.'

'And what did she say to that?'

'She said that when true love comes along, you should grab it with both hands and not let go.' Fletcher shook his head slowly. 'I was a fool, Molly, because I let you go all those years ago. I made so many terrible mistakes back then and I've spent a long time regretting them.'

'Then why didn't you contact me sooner?' She paced around the garden. 'Why wait until you meet another woman, accept her proposal because you were lonely, then when you have to do legal paperwork only then discover that you're still married to someone else? If you really wanted me, why not come and get me?'

'I wanted to. So many times, Molly, but—'

'But? But, what?'

'But I didn't think you'd ever forgive me.'

She opened her eyes wider at that. 'Forgive you?'

'Katie.' The one word was soft, barely audible but Molly heard it loud and clear and it pierced her heart. She winced and nodded.

'Katie.'

'I was a beast, Molly. I was—'

'We've already gone over this, haven't we?' She held up her hands. 'It was a long time ago. We've both changed.'

'But her memory, that whole situation, it's still between us.'

'It'll always be between us, Fletcher. We were her parents.' Molly sighed and sat on the bench near the flower garden her brother-in-law had planted, her coffee forgotten. Thankfully, Fletcher didn't come and sit next to her. Instead he stood nearby, looking at the rabbits as they nibbled the grass, their noses twitching.

'They're so content.'

'Yes.'

'And when I saw them jumping over their barrier things that Lydia and George set up, they seemed happy.' He chuckled. 'I don't know how I know that. Perhaps I'm just projecting my own thoughts onto the situation. I was happy watching them so I'm presuming the rabbits were happy being harnessed and led over a series of jumps.'

'Perhaps you actually saw one of them smile,' she remarked, a touch of humour in her tone. Fletcher looked over at her and smiled.

'Why do we complicate everything so much? Why can't everything be straightforward?' He walked towards her and sat down but made no effort to touch her.

'Because then life would be boring.'

'True.' He nodded in agreement, then shifted to face her. 'Life was never boring with you.'

'We did have a lot of ups and downs.'

'The ups were good, though. Weren't they?'

Molly nodded. 'They definitely were.' Her gaze dropped to his mouth, memories of exactly how good things had been between them springing instantly to mind.

'Molly, don't look at me like that.' His words were quiet, deep and filled with repressed desire.

'We've been here before. Several times in fact,'

she whispered. 'Staring at each other. The atmosphere around us forming a bubble where only the two of us exist.'

He edged a little closer, his body angling more towards hers. He raised his hand and brushed her hair behind her ear. She hadn't moved, hadn't tried to shift away. Not this time. He swallowed, knowing a lot was riding on this moment. He didn't want to spook her, didn't want to pressure her but he wasn't sure he could resist her any longer.

'You're not spooking me,' she whispered and it was only then that Fletch realised he'd spoken the last part out loud. 'And I'm not sure I want you to resist,' she continued, her words music to his ears.

'Molly? Are you sure?'

'That I want to kiss you?' She closed her eyes, her body leaning slightly towards him. 'That I want you to kiss me back?' She looked at him, desperation, need and longing in her tone. 'Oh, yes, Fletcher. I want that. I need that—right now.'

Her last two words were soft and accompanied by an irresistible, sensual tremor. No man in his right mind could fight the temptation any longer and, with one swift move, he slipped his arms about her, drawing her close, before lowering his head to capture her lips in a kiss so intensely powerful, he felt as though the earth had literally shifted beneath them.

She tasted exactly as he'd remembered except *more so*. All he wanted was to have her as close to him as possible, to ravage her, to put his mark upon her skin. She was his. She'd always been his and he couldn't believe how animalistic, how primal she was making him feel. He'd never counted himself as a possessive man, in fact, he'd always thought he was quite the opposite, but not around Molly. She was *his* Molly. She always had been and always would be.

He forced himself to slow down, to take the time to reacquaint himself with every contour of her lips, the curve of her cheek, the dip of her chin. He brought one hand up to her face, to feel that silky smoothness of her skin. He eased his mouth from hers for the briefest of seconds, both of them sucking in a breath as he tenderly trailed the pad of his thumb across her parted lips, and was delighted when a sensual tremor passed through her body.

She was with him. She was right there in the moment. He wasn't alone with all these over-powering and conflicting emotions. He wanted her. She wanted him. They had a history, a past, but it had always been this way between them, so perfect, so necessary, so right.

This time, when he retouched his lips to hers, he had himself better under control. He wanted to show Molly just how much he cherished her, how beautiful she was, how he appreciated her for who she was, the physical, the mental and the emotional. He didn't just want one part of her, he wanted them all. She'd been able to give herself to him before—would she be able to do that now?

Soft and smooth and slow. He wanted to savour everything, to blend the memories of the past with the memories of the present. She'd changed, matured, her mouth a little more plump than all those years ago, but that only made it that much more exciting to kiss.

When he opened his mouth, she did the same, granting him whatever access he wanted, and once more he had to ignore the surge of desire, of excitement, of possession that pulsed through him. She ran her tongue across his lower lip and he moaned with delight. How could he have forgotten just how quickly she could tie him in knots with the simplest of intimate touches?

She then surprised him by taking the initiative and slowing the kiss down even more, heightening the sensuality surrounding them. It was as though they were the only two people on earth. No one else mattered. Nothing else mattered, except for here and now. Him and her. She plunged her fingers into his hair, holding his head in place as she nibbled and teased and sighed with longing.

He slid his arm more firmly around her, wanting her as close as possible. Now that he'd tasted her, touched her, breathed her in, he wasn't sure he was able to stop, wasn't able to keep things at this slow and sensual pace as his longing for her intensified with every passing second. The animal began to return and she allowed it. When he broke his mouth from hers to place hot and desperate kisses along her cheek, travelling down her neck, she tilted her head back, granting him whatever access he desired.

Then, as though she was as impatient as him, she urged his head back up, back towards her mouth, and this time the heat and fire were un-leashed, both of them surrendering to the moment. Would he ever be able to get enough of her? He'd thought he'd managed to get over her all those years ago. He'd been wrong. So very wrong.

'Why did we ever get divorced?' He growled against her lips, his breathing erratic, before he captured them once more.

We didn't, she answered him silently.

'You're so addictive,' he murmured between kisses.

Molly was unable to respond because all she could concentrate on was the way she felt in Fletcher's arms. He tasted exactly the same, his scent was the one that excited her the most, his tender, caring touch was just as she'd remembered. How could he be so different and yet so familiar?

'Fletch.' Even his name fitted perfectly on her lips as she kissed him once, twice, three times again, her breath coming in short bursts. 'Oxygen,' she managed to get out. 'Necessary.'

His answer was a soft, sexy chuckle, one that did nothing to stop the mounting desire flooding throughout her entire body. 'It's OK. I'm a doctor. I know how to revive someone.' He kissed her again, his lips possessive on hers before he nuzzled her neck, planting more kisses there as Molly gasped for air.

'How is it possible?' she whispered between breaths, her hands coming to rest at the back of his neck.

'What?' He continued to spread small kisses down her neck, stopping momentarily to nibble on her ear.

'Us.'

'I know.' Fletch lifted his head and gazed longingly into her eyes. 'You are still so incredibly stunning, Molly.'

She smiled shyly at his words but couldn't believe how lovely it was to hear him say such wonderful things to her. It made her feel free. Fighting the attraction to him had clearly been causing her far more stress than she'd realised and now that that pressure had been released, she was going to ride the wave of euphoria for as long as possible.

'I'm serious. That's not just a line I'm feeding you.' He brushed a few more kisses across her lips and she responded with longing. 'You'll always be this beautiful to me.' He tucked her hair behind her ear once more. 'Even when we're old and grey.'

'What?' The world around them shattered back into reality and she eased back from his arms. 'What do you mean?'

Fletcher looked at her as though she'd just grown an extra head. He dropped his hands and shifted a little in order to see her more clearly. 'That kiss we just shared…' He gestured to the small amount of space between them. 'That isn't normal for everyone, you know. What we have between us is…magnificent, Molly. Surely you realise that.'

Her gaze dropped to his mouth, as though she wanted nothing more than to repeat it. 'Yes, I do but it's always been that way between us. The physical attraction has never been an issue for us, even right from the beginning. It was why we fought so hard against it for most of our overseas trip, unsure how to deal with all those hormones and pheromones.'

'We were fools.'

'We were being cautious, becoming friends.'

She stood and walked over to the flower box where he'd put their drinks, staring down at the now cold liquid. If she continued to be near him, continued to look at him with his slightly mussed dark hair and come-to-bed eyes, there was no telling what might happen.

'True but when we finally gave in to the attraction, to those feelings, it was good, Molly. You have to admit it.'

'It was better than good, Fletch.' She glanced at him over her shoulder, giving him a look that said he didn't need to state the obvious.

He walked over to her and took her gently in his arms once more, pleased when she didn't resist. He lowered his head to brush a tantalising kiss across her lips, in the way he knew she liked. He knew so much about her and he was clearly using it to his advantage. She did like it when he kissed her neck, when he ran his fingers through her crazy curls, when he gazed into her eyes as though she really were the most important person in the world.

'Fletch.' She breathed his name, the sound holding a mix of longing, need and regret as she twisted from his touch. 'Fletch, stop.' Again her words were whispered, as though she was half begging for more, half uncertain about exactly what she wanted. 'What did you mean before? About growing old and grey? Surely you don't mean we should stay married, do you?'

'Why not?'

'What?' Her eyebrows shot up and her eyes widened. She pulled back and moved away from him, her mind whirling, her body flooding with repressed desire. How was she supposed to think clearly when he was so near, so enticing, so… Fletch. 'You can't be serious.'

'We belong together.' His tone was imploring. 'After everything we've been through, we've come full circle. We're compatible in so many ways and I…' He swallowed, unsure if it was too soon to confess just how much he loved her. He stepped forward and Molly stepped backwards, putting up her hands to stop him but she simply came into contact with firm, muscled torso, the one her fingertips knew every inch of and now tingled to explore once more. Fletch cupped her face in his hands and stared into her eyes, his words soft and heartfelt.

'My life without you is—'

'Fletcher—*don't.*' Molly swallowed, her heart pounding beneath her ribs, wanting to agree with him, to throw caution to the wind, but knowing she couldn't. Too much had happened between them, too many things had been said and left unsaid. Although she knew it sounded great, although she'd often dreamed of getting back together with Fletcher, she also knew it wasn't that simple.

'Molly…you must know how I feel about you.'

'Do I?' She closed her eyes, knowing that if she looked at him, she might crumble, give in to the physical urgings. They'd tried marriage and they'd failed. There was no way she could fail again. Not with Fletcher. Not with anyone. It had taken her such a long time to get over him and move on with her life that she just couldn't…she couldn't go back.

'Yes.'

She reached for logic, for reason, for rationality. It was the only defence she could muster when he was this close to her. 'Fletch, only yesterday evening you were engaged to another woman.' She spread her arms wide.

'While I was still married to you,' he added,

exasperation in his tone. 'I know this whole situation isn't ideal but at least it's proved one thing.'

'What's that?'

'That the past is the past. We can't change it but this—this thing which still exists between us—we can make it work. You and me.'

'How?' She wrenched from his touch and headed towards the back gate. 'I—this is all just too much, too soon. It's crazy talk.'

'No, it's not.'

'Yes, it is, Fletcher. Of course we're good together. We always have been and I know we can't change the past. I know that but that doesn't mean I can just forget it. I won't forget it. I won't forget *her.*'

'I'm not asking you to but, Molly, this is our chance to start over. To have the family we'd always talked about.'

'You do want to have children. I knew it.' She unlatched the gate and stepped through. 'It didn't work out with Eliza and so I'm the next candidate in line.'

'Molly. No.' Her words cut him deeply and for a split second she paused, regret crossing her face. 'Please?' He held out a hand to her. 'Come back. Let's sit and talk this through.'

'No.' She shook her head, her voice catching as the emotions started to come to the surface. 'I can't. It's all just…too much.' With that, she turned and all but sprinted down the side path of the house.

Fletcher watched her go, his heart beginning to ache with a pain he hadn't felt in such a long time. He'd thought it would all work out. He'd thought if he could kiss her, get her to feel what he knew still existed between them, then she'd come around to his way of thinking.

He felt guilty about the past but he meant what he'd said, he couldn't change it. He could, however, learn from it, but, even if she told him that she forgave him for the past, would he ever really be able to forgive himself?

He walked towards the gate and looked down the path. She'd gone. His beautiful, wonderful, sexy Molly had gone…and he had no idea if he'd ever really win her back.

CHAPTER TWELVE

THE REST OF Sunday passed in a blur. By the time she'd returned from her impromptu run, she'd been even more on edge than before. Thankfully, the family had returned and the house was alive with voices and activity. Molly listened intently to Lydia as she talked about her rabbit. George wanted his big sister's attention with his maths homework and Molly was only too happy to hide out in his room helping him.

Pierce's sister, Nell, allowed Molly to help with her latest jigsaw puzzle and Jasmine had questions about her biology presentation. Between reading stories to Ty, chatting with her brothers-in-law and ignoring concerned glances from Stacey and Cora, Molly did very well in avoiding being alone with Fletcher. That was, until it was time for them to leave.

She'd delayed their departure for as long as possible, insisting they stay for the evening meal so that neither of them would have to worry about it when they finally got home. Fletcher, thankfully, had instantly agreed and she'd wondered whether he was as nervous about the drive home together as she was.

'I'm happy to drive,' she said as she finished saying goodbye to her family.

'You drove here. It's only fair I drive home,' Fletcher said, walking around and getting into the driver's seat. Molly closed her eyes and counted to ten.

'Count to twenty,' Cora commented close by and Molly opened her eyes and threw her arms around her sister's neck.

'I don't want to get in the car with him,' she confessed. 'I'm sure he wants to continue talking about…about…and I don't know if I'm ready. It's just too much, too soon. Isn't it?'

'It's less than two hours and there shouldn't be too much traffic so you'll be fine,' Cora soothed, patting Molly on the back. 'You're an awesome, caring and loving person, Molly, and whatever he might say or ask you, you'll handle it. You're brilliant. Remember that. You take after your sisters.'

Molly grinned at that and looked at Cora.

'Besides, Stacey and I will be thinking of you, sending you all our best thoughts through the invisible triplet bond we share.'

Molly chuckled. 'You always know just what to say,' she remarked.

'That's because we're connected.' Cora hugged her once more before Molly opened her arms and beckoned Stacey over, the three of them standing there with their arms around each other in a little circle.

'It's not that far,' Molly whispered.

'That's right,' Stacey encouraged. 'Just keep on talking things out with him and you'll have it all sorted in no time at all.'

'She was talking about the drive back,' Cora pointed out with a chuckle. 'But Stace does have a point.'

'Hey.' Molly glared at them both. 'You're supposed to be on *my* side.'

'We are!' they said in unison before hugging her once more.

'Get going,' Stacey said.

'Call us when you get in,' Cora added, and Molly reluctantly walked to the car, waving once more before opening the passenger side door.

'Is it difficult? Leaving your family, especially Stacey and Cora? I know how close you three are.'

'Not really. I'll talk to them on the phone to-night to let them know we've arrived safely but we're sort of used to being parted. Cora spends a good deal of time in Tarparnii each year. Stacey and Pierce travel to the States and the UK quite often for Pierce to present papers at conferences.'

'Ah, yes. He mentioned his speciality was in-tegration into society for adults with Asperger's and autism. Quite enlightening.'

'So going back to Sydney, which is only a short drive from home, isn't really that difficult to bear.'

'Good.' He nodded and glanced her way but she kept her eyes fixed straight ahead. 'Good,' he repeated, returning his attention to the road. Where the silence between them had previously been one of comfort and ease, this one was the complete opposite, making Molly feel stifled and edgy. She quickly flicked on the radio, prefer-ring to listen to a talk-back station so she didn't have to talk at all to Fletcher. He seemed fine with this, in so much as he didn't try to turn it off and talk to her about what had happened between them.

Molly closed her eyes and rested her head back against the head rest as the artificial glow from the street lights flashed by, illuminating them for a second or two before the next one in line took over.

Fletch wanted to stay married to her. He didn't want to get divorced. He wanted to try again. He wanted to have children! He'd broken his engagement with Eliza because he had feelings for her. That was huge. It was all so huge and life changing and she already had so much to contend with at work and her studies and…was it any wonder her thoughts were in complete turmoil?

And children! Could she do that? Could she open herself up to those emotions again? She'd locked away her maternal instincts and focused on her career, on her patients. What she'd been through during her pregnancy, feeling Katie moving inside her, loving every new sensation— could she do that again? What if…what if something bad happened again?

A fresh bout of tears began forming behind her eyes and she quickly forced herself not to think about it. Trying not to sniff lest Fletcher should start asking her questions, wanting to know if she was all right, Molly shifted slightly and focused on listening to what the radio announcer was saying.

It wasn't until they'd pulled up outside the house, Fletcher turning off the engine, that he spoke into the now silent atmosphere around them.

'Molly, we need to talk.'

'Not now.'

'No. Not now but soon. I know you have a lot to think about, as do I, but—'

'Fletcher.' She held up both her hands and bit her lip. 'Don't. *Please*. This past week has been a roller coaster of emotions and right now I don't have any more to give.'

He hesitated for a moment before agreeing. 'OK.' He nodded once, then opened the door and climbed from the car. He retrieved their bags, then walked up the path towards the duplex. She stood beside him on their shared front porch. Him in front of his door. Her in front of hers. They both put their keys in the locks and opened the doors.

'Thanks for driving,' she murmured.

Fletcher forced a smile. 'Thanks for taking me to see your family again. I really did have a relaxing break. It was just what I needed.'

When she smiled this time, it was genuine. 'I'm glad.'

'Goodnight, Molly. Sleep sweet.'

'You, too.' She headed inside and locked the door behind her before reaching for her phone and calling her sisters. Neither of them tried to get her to talk about the drive, neither of them pressed her to discuss what had happened earlier that day. All they did was reassure her that they were always there for her, no matter what, and that whenever she wanted to talk both of them would be ready to listen.

As Molly went through the motions of getting ready for bed, setting her alarm and brushing her teeth, she looked at the teddy bear sitting on her dresser. Katie's teddy bear. She picked it up and carried it to the bed, sliding between the covers and cuddling the bear close. Her Katie. Her beautiful Katie was gone.

'Is it possible, Katie?' she whispered into the dark. 'Is it possible for us all to be happy?'

No answers came and, through sheer exhaustion, Molly drifted off to sleep.

When she woke the next morning, she still felt the heavy weight hanging around her neck. She didn't want to feel like this. She didn't want to have these decisions to make. Not now. Not when her life was already filled with the stress of finishing her studies and doing final exams.

As she ate her breakfast, she looked at the documents Stacey had given her, the ones the lawyers had sent her all those years ago. She read the letter explaining that sections of the documents hadn't been correctly signed, that the divorce wouldn't be final until that occurred.

She really was still married to Fletcher. She was his wife and a part of her just wanted to fling her arms about his neck, press her lips to his and tell him that she wanted to be with him for ever, that she wanted to start their marriage afresh, that she wanted to try again to have children and to be the happy family she'd dreamed about all those years ago.

But it just wasn't that simple. Life never was.

When she stepped out of her front door, she half expected Fletcher to be waiting for her on the porch, but he wasn't. As she walked along the footpath towards the hospital she half expected him to come up behind her, but he didn't. As she entered the surgical wards she half expected him to be standing at the nurses' station, chatting amicably with the staff, but there was no sign of him.

'Uh…has…um…Fletcher been in this morning?' she asked the ward sister but the other woman shook her head. 'OK. Thanks.' Molly continued on with her duties, doing a quick ward round, checking on her patients before heading to Theatres for the morning list.

She focused on work. Theatre was running late due to a complication with her fourth patient. Afterwards, she went to clinic and worked her way through the plethora of patients waiting to see her. There was still no sign of Fletcher. Alexis hadn't seen him and when she checked on Mr Majors, she was told that Fletcher had called to say he wouldn't be in today.

Frowning at this news, Molly returned to her office. Was he at home? Was he ill? She hoped not. Why hadn't he come in today? Was it his scheduled day off? Knowing there was no point in playing twenty questions by herself, she forced herself to concentrate. By the end of the day, when she'd finished dictating a load of letters and catching up on the never-ending paperwork, she finally made her way back home.

The hire car wasn't parked outside the house so she presumed he'd returned it. She started making dinner but after a while stopped and actually went to the connecting wall between their places and listened. She closed her eyes, listening for any sounds from next door but, apart from a ticking clock, there was nothing.

Where was he? She'd tried to casually ask several people but no one had seen him.

'Perhaps he had a day off,' Cora said later that evening when Molly called her sisters over the Internet chat.

'Maybe he kept the hire car and went for a drive,' Stacey added.

'Yeah.' Molly sighed. 'I just can't help but feel as though he's avoiding me.'

'Wasn't that what you were planning to do to him?' Stacey's eyebrows rose. 'Perhaps he's giving you both some time to think about things.'

'What exactly did he say to rile you up?' Cora wanted to know. 'Because the only thing I can think of is that he told you he doesn't want to get divorced after all. That he wants to stay married.'

'Bingo!' Molly shrugged one shoulder.

Cora laughed triumphantly. 'The triplet bond strikes again.'

'Well, I think that's marvellous,' Stacey added, laughing along with Cora. 'The two of you are perfect for each other.'

'You always have been.'

'Even just watching the two of you this weekend,' Stacey continued, 'it was as though our family was...' She shrugged, trying to find the right word.

'Complete,' Cora finished for her.

'Yeah. Complete.'

'But what about...everything? He wants to settle down here and have children.'

'He does! That's fantastic.' Stacey, the real homebody out of the three of them, was clearly delighted with this prospect.

'I want to travel, to do something with my new qualifications, to make a difference.'

'You need to have this conversation with him.' Cora's tone was firm. 'You need to tell him how you feel, Molly. That's the only way this is going to get sorted out because it's as clear to Stacey and I as it is to you—although you probably can't admit it right now—that you're still one hundred per cent in love with him.'

'Well, of course I am.' Molly threw her arms in the air in utter exasperation. 'I always have been and I always will be. He's *Fletch* but I was in love with him before and it still didn't work out. I didn't get my happily ever after. What if that happens again? What if we still can't make it work? I just don't think I can recover from the pain of losing him again.'

Molly reached for a tissue and dabbed the tears that had somehow started trickling down her cheeks. She blew her nose and shrugged. 'What am I supposed to do? What if I get pregnant again and lose the baby again? What if Fletcher reacts the way he did last time? Can I trust him to be there for me? To support me?'

'I thought you'd forgiven him for the way he behaved?' Stacey asked.

'Oh, I have, but that still doesn't mean I'm not nervous or worried or freaked out. He just started talking about settling down and starting a family and, hey, we can do that straight away because we're still legally married.'

'And your biological clock is ticking,' Cora pointed out, a light-hearted tone to her words.

Molly grimaced and buried her head in her hands. 'I know all these things but I have exams, I have my own plans and now he's just come back into my life, turned it all upside down and made me question myself and I hate questioning myself.'

'We know.' Stacey smiled.

'But at the end of the day…I mean…he's…he's Fletcher.' When she spoke his name, she felt the anxiety starting to dissipate. '*My* Fletcher.'

'Talk to him, Molly,' Stacey urged.

'Give him a call,' Cora added.

'Do you think he'd mind? Me calling him? Asking him where he is? Why he didn't turn up to the hospital today?'

Cora's grin was wide. 'You're his wife, aren't you?'

'Call him,' Stacey reiterated.

'It'll work out,' Cora implored. 'Trust us.'

Molly sniffed and nodded. 'OK. I'll call him.'

After ending the Internet chat to her sisters,

Molly looked at her cell phone. 'Just ring him. Just ring him.' She paced around the room, sighing repeatedly as she worked up the nerve to call him. 'Just ring him.' She looked at her phone, then, before she could deliberate any more, she pressed the button to connect the call.

'You can do this. You can do this.' The phone rang a few times but he didn't answer. When she realised it was going to go through to voicemail, she quickly tried to construct what she was going to say. The beep sounded…and for a moment she froze. Feeling like an idiot, she disconnected the call, then began agitatedly pacing again.

'No. Molly. Stop being stupid. This is Fletcher. Just Fletcher. It's OK.' Taking a deep breath, she redialled his number, thinking clearly what she would say when the beep sounded.

'Hi. It's Molly. Sorry about that last call. Got cut off. Not sure what happened. Listen…uh… can you…uh…give me a call? Thanks.'

She disconnected the call, proud of herself. Now all she had to do was to wait. 'And that isn't going to be easy,' she remarked as she headed into the kitchen because she needed to be doing *something*. She knew it was impossible to settle her mind down to any sort of paperwork so decided to bake some scones.

'It's quite normal,' she told herself, 'to be baking at this time of night. Nothing wrong with it at all.' She kept glancing at her phone, hoping it didn't ring when she had her hands covered in flour kneading the dough. It didn't. She hoped it wouldn't ring when she had the oven gloves on, pulling the hot scones from the oven. It didn't. She really hoped it didn't ring when she had her mouth stuffed full with scones, jam and cream. It didn't.

She also kept listening, waiting for any sorts of sounds from next door, but there was nothing. Once, she thought she heard him on the front porch but when she rushed to the door and opened it to check, a bright smile on her face, her heart sank when she realised it was just a cat.

Should she call him again? She pondered the question as she cleaned up the kitchen. What if he'd been in some sort of accident? What if he really wasn't well and was doubled over in pain or needed help? Her imagination started to slip into overdrive and she instantly picked up the phone and called him again.

'Hi, Fletch. Me again,' she said to his voice-mail. 'Starting to get a little worried that you haven't received my messages. If you don't want to talk to me, then at least just send me a text message so I know you're OK. You know me. I worry. Right. Bye.'

She disconnected the call then waited once more, almost willing the phone to ring. When it didn't, she decided to at least try and get a bit of studying done and actually managed to work for a good hour but still he hadn't called. It was now two o'clock in the morning and she hoped that, wherever he was, he was sleeping but, being a surgeon, he might have gone to the hospital to help out for some strange reason. She called the hospital switchboard and asked if Fletcher was in the hospital. The operator tried several different wards before letting her know that she couldn't find him and suggested Molly try his cell phone.

'Thanks.' Molly hung up and tried to think of where else Fletcher might have gone. 'All day long!' Perhaps it was as Stacey had said and he'd kept the hire car and gone for a drive somewhere. If so, he could be anywhere. He could have driven down to Melbourne to see Eliza, to tell her he'd made a mistake, that he did still want to divorce Molly.

At that thought, she broke down in tears and stood from her desk to go and lie down on her bed, hugging Katie bear close. Why was she so upset at the thought of him going back to Eliza? That had been his plan all along. To get her to sign the divorce papers and to marry Eliza. Why should it bother her so much *now*?

'Because you love him, you idiot. You really, really, really love him and you don't want to be divorced from him and you do want the chance to start again but there are…there are…so many things to talk about and…where is he?'

Molly sobbed into her pillow, feeling utterly miserable. Katie bear was in her arms and her cell phone was in her hand, ready and waiting to answer as soon as he called. She sniffed a little, then rang his number again, not caring at all about the time. 'Fletch? Fletch?' She sniffed into the phone, angst in her tone. 'Where are you? Are you OK? I'm worried, Fletch. Please call me. I just need to know you're OK. Please. Please call me.' With a broken sob, she disconnected the call and waited.

Closing her eyes, she tried to calm her breathing. He was all right. He had to be all right. They'd found each other again and so it would be an incredibly cruel thing to happen if he was… if he'd been…

No. She wouldn't think about it. She couldn't. He was fine. He was fine.

'He's fine,' she whispered to Katie bear before slipping off into a restless sleep.

She awoke to sunlight twinkling gently in through her window and a pounding in her head. She looked at the clock and realised it was a quarter to six. Then she realised that the pounding wasn't only in her head but that someone was at her front door…knocking quite loudly.

'Molly?' Fletcher's deep voice boomed through the wooden door.

Springing from the bed, she ran to the door, belatedly realising she was still holding the teddy bear. She flung open the door and, when she saw him standing on the other side, she all but flung herself into his arms. 'You're OK. You're OK.' She held him tight, never wanting to let him go again. 'I thought you were… I was worried and I… When I couldn't get any answer…' She broke off, knowing her words were incoherent and mumbled against his neck. Somehow Fletcher shifted so that he was now standing inside her hallway and closed the door behind them.

'Molly? What's happened?' He eased her back a little and looked into her tear-stained face, instantly brushing a thumb across her cheek, the touch tender and caring.

'You weren't answering your phone. I was so worried.'

'It ran out of battery. Sorry. I went for a drive yesterday to clear my head, to think things through and I didn't charge my phone or have a signal.'

'So you didn't get any of my messages?' Molly dropped her hands from his neck, feeling a little embarrassed. It was only then he saw the bear in her hands. He pointed.

'Is that…?'

'Katie bear.' Molly nodded. 'I was worried last night.'

'So I'm beginning to understand.'

'Hang on.' She looked at him with confusion. 'If you didn't get my messages, then why were you just pounding on my door?'

It was his turn to look a little sheepish. 'I spent most of yesterday at the beach, walking along the sand, thinking, trying to figure out what to do next and all I could come up with was to just let you know that I'll do anything you want. If you want to get divorced, then that's what we'll do. Whatever happens between us, Molly, what matters most to me is your happiness.'

'Really?'

'Yes.' He nodded and looked down at the teddy bear again, reaching out and taking it from her hands. 'We have so much history between us.'

'Yes.' She jerked her thumb over her shoulder, indicating the lounge room. 'Let's have a seat, eh?'

'Good idea.'

'Where did you stay last night? I didn't hear you come home.'

A small smile touched his lips. 'Were you waiting up for me?'

'Yes. I was worried.'

'Oh. Again, sorry. I walked a long way at the beach, thinking and trying to figure things out, and I was just exhausted. I stopped at a hotel by the beach and left there about half an hour ago, wanting to miss the peak-hour traffic. I didn't mean to pound on the door but the urgency of the situation, of what I wanted to say to you, it just surged through me.'

Molly sat next to him on the lounge and brushed her fingers through his hair. 'I'm glad you're OK.' Relief was starting to flood through her, making her feel more exhausted than if she'd been in Theatre all night long. 'So what is it you want to say to me?'

'Hmm. Yes. Good.' He chuckled. 'It all sounded so perfect in my head, so rational, so relevant, but I guess the upshot of the whole thing is…' Fletcher looked directly into her eyes and slowly exhaled '…I still love you, Molly. Very much.'

Her breath caught in her throat at his words and her heart sang with delight. 'You do?'

'Yes.' He cupped her cheek, his touch tender.

'And you're serious about…about everything you said back in Newcastle?'

'That I want to settle down with you and create a family of our own?'

She nodded.

'Yes. If it's what you want.'

Molly closed her eyes for a moment. 'What if

it's not what I want?' Fletch dropped his hands and she looked at him once more.

'What do you want? Not only for us but for you? What do *you* want, Molly?'

'I want to get through my exams. To qualify. To travel overseas and work. I can't do that if I'm pregnant or lugging a baby or two around.'

He started to laugh and she glared at him. 'This isn't funny, Fletcher.'

'No. No, it isn't,' he responded, quickly covering over his mirth. 'I was just imagining you, like the native women of Tarparnii, walking around with a baby strapped to your back while you visit patients.'

Molly's indignation dissipated and she rolled her eyes. 'You know what I'm talking about.'

'Yes. I really do.'

'And you were the one who arrived at Sydney General to encourage qualified surgeons to head overseas to countries where medical help isn't readily available.'

'I did do that.'

'And do you really, *really* want to settle down in suburbia? Going to a big teaching hospital, doing the same thing, day in, day out?'

'When you say it like that, it doesn't sound appealing at all.' He leaned closer and gazed into her eyes once more, sighing with pure contentment.

'So you do want to travel some more?'

'Molly...' he took her hand in his '...I want to be where you are. If we're travelling, then we're travelling. If we're living next door to Stacey, then that's where we'll be.' He kissed her hand then brushed a kiss across her lips. 'I let you go once before and it was the biggest mistake of my life. I should have fought harder, I should have compromised more, I should have listened—*really* listened to what you were saying.'

'Thank you, Fletch.' She pressed her mouth to his, wanting to show him just how much she did appreciate his words. 'Thank you for listening. It means a lot.'

'And you forgive me? For the things I said all those years ago? I was...' He closed his eyes. 'I'm ashamed of what I said.'

Molly touched the side of his face and he opened his eyes. 'Of course I forgive you. It wasn't an easy time for either of us.'

He nodded but she could still see his pain. 'Have you forgiven yourself?'

Fletch shook his head. 'It's not important.'

'Actually, it is. If we're going to be able to move forward, we need to leave everything in the past.' Even as she spoke the words it was as though she was telling herself the same thing.

'You want a new beginning?'

She shook her head. 'I like the beginning we have but we need to…to…not be so harsh on ourselves. Let the angst and the pressure we had back then go. Forgive yourself for your behaviour because only then can we really bond.' Her tone was earnest, her heart filling with a renewed sense of confidence.

She kissed him again and this time he shifted closer, pulling her onto his lap. There was no way Molly was going to protest because she wanted to be with Fletcher as much as he wanted to be with her.

'You mean a lot to me,' he whispered some time later, his breathing as erratic as hers.

'I'm sure you'll show me just how much.' She winked at him and he laughed.

'Oh, I've missed you, Molly. No one understands me the way you do.' He shifted around for a moment and she wondered if she was hurting him but he shook his head. 'It's fine.' He paused, his expression growing serious once more. 'Molly, if you want to travel—and I completely understand that—what would that mean with regards to children? Because I do want children and I want to have children with you.' Fletcher reached for Katie bear and stroked the satin ribbon.

Molly closed her eyes, knowing she needed to concentrate but finding it increasingly difficult with the love of her life so close. She was still delighting in the fact that she had every right in the world to touch him, to kiss him, to offer her love to him and not have it rejected. 'In Newcastle, when you mentioned having a family…uh…I… There's something I need to tell you.'

'You don't want children?' His tone wasn't critical or condescending, merely concerned.

Molly opened her eyes and brushed a kiss over his mouth. 'It's not that I don't want them, it's just that…I'm…I'm really scared.'

'Scared?'

'What if what happened to Katie happens to

the next baby, or the next?' She spread her arms wide, her voice catching in her throat. 'What if there's something wrong between us and we… we can't…*I* can't carry a baby to full term?'

'You're scared of getting pregnant again?'

Molly nodded, unable to completely voice her fears. 'And I'm not getting any younger,' she pointed out. 'Which means, as far as conception and carrying a child, the risks become even greater. I don't want to disappoint you or let you down again. I don't want to let myself down again.'

'You won't. You can't. We're in this together, Molly, and I think you need to forgive yourself just as much as I need to forgive myself.' He shook his head. 'We were different people back then. We've had more life experience now, grown, changed.' He brushed her hair back behind her ear, caressing her cheek with his fingers. 'We do need to let go and I think we can help each other to do so.' He kissed her softly. 'What happened all those years ago, with our gorgeous little girl, the chances of it happening again are extremely slim.'

'But—' Molly sniffed a little, her eyes starting

to brim with tears. 'What if it does happen? I really am scared, Fletcher.' Her lower lip began to wobble. 'I don't think I'm strong enough to go through all of that again. It broke my heart the first time and…and…'

He pressed his lips to hers, wanting to reassure her, to encourage her and to make a promise.

'Whatever happens,' he whispered as he brushed a tear from her lashes with his thumb, 'then we'll face it. *Together.*'

'You won't leave me to cope alone?'

'No. I was such a fool. I was selfish, inexperienced with life, even though I thought I knew everything. You had clearly bonded with Katie, feeling her kick inside you, listening to her heart beat at your check-up appointments. All I could think about was the job offers that were coming in and wanting you by my side so we could jump-start our life together.'

'We were so young.'

'Yes. It didn't seem so at the time but, we were.'

'I do want children, Fletch.' She sniffed and nodded, blinking the threatening tears away. 'I do. But at the moment—'

'You want your career more,' he stated. 'You

want to help, to make a difference, to save the world.' He chuckled as he spoke, slipping his arms further around her, keeping her where she most needed to be—with him.

'So long as I can save the world with you.'

'It's a date.' He kissed her, then just sat there for a long moment, the two of them more content than they'd been in years.

'Do you know, Stacey thinks you're the missing piece to our family puzzle.'

'Does she now? Isn't that nice?'

'You are. She's definitely right there.'

'I really enjoyed seeing everyone and meeting new people. I loved it.'

'Me, too.'

'Except for the last bit.'

'I didn't know how to tell you that I…I wasn't sure about having children, that I was scared… well, terrified, really. I thought you might take back what you'd said, about not wanting to get divorced.'

'No.' He shook his head very slowly from side to side. 'Whether we have children or not isn't what this is about, Molly. It's about you and I. It's about the two of us being together—for ever.'

And with that, he picked up Katie bear and held her out to Molly. She smiled and stroked the bear's fur, then the old satin ribbon and it was then…she saw a diamond ring tied to the ribbon.

'What the—' She looked from the ring to Fletcher and back again, her fingers gently touching the most perfect ring she'd ever seen.

'We never really got you an engagement ring all those years ago. It's another thing I want to rectify.'

'How—'

'I'm a magician, remember.' He winked at her as he carefully undid the knot of ribbon around the ring. He reached for her left hand and as he slid the ring into place, the magnificent piece of jewellery fitting her finger perfectly, he kissed her and whispered, 'Molly Wilton, will you marry me…again?'

'Yes.' It didn't matter that, legally, they were already married. What mattered was the connecting of their hearts, their minds and their souls.

'I love you,' he whispered against her lips.

'I love you, too,' she returned, kissing him again and again. As she sighed with utter contentment she eased back to look at him. 'How *did* you get the ring onto the ribbon without me seeing?'

Fletcher tapped the side of his nose twice. 'A magician never reveals his secrets.'

'Is that so?'

'Uh-huh.'

'I'll get you to talk.'

'Not going to happen.'

'Yes, it will, because I have a few tricks of my own up my sleeve.'

'Oh, yeah?' He was clearly intrigued. 'What's that?'

Molly eased herself from his lap, then held out her hand to him. 'Why don't you come into the bedroom, my wonderful husband, and I'll show you?'

'You think you can get me to reveal my secrets?' He linked his fingers with hers and stood up.

'I do.'

'Then let's get started. I have a feeling your methods might be quite…exhilarating.'

Molly's answer was to laugh, a laugh that resounded through the walls, filling the area around them with pure happiness.

EPILOGUE

ONE WEEK AFTER Molly's final exams, she and Fletcher headed to Newcastle to celebrate with the family. No sooner had they pulled into the driveway than Stacey and Cora came running down the side path of the house, eager to see her.

'I'll grab the bags and go find the blokes,' Fletcher remarked, giving her a quick kiss before Molly was whisked into a firm embrace by her oldest sister.

'I'm so proud of you,' Stacey said. 'Mr Molly Wilton.'

Cora laughed at Stacey's comment. 'That's right. I'd forgotten that when you become a surgeon, you become a "Mr".'

'I think I might stick with doctor, if you don't mind.' Molly hugged both her sisters close, the three of them taking a moment to just relax and silently celebrate their accomplishments together.

'Dad and Tish would have been so proud of you,' Stacey said after a moment.

'They would have been proud of all of us. Jasmine, George and Lydia included,' Molly stated.

'I'm sure they're looking down on us,' Cora added as Jasmine came running in their direction, her arms open wide.

'My turn for a sisterly hug.' She laughed and the three older siblings enfolded her into their hug.

'I love my family,' Molly murmured and her sisters agreed.

'What's going on here?' They all looked over their shoulder to see Lydia standing there glaring at them with her hands on her hips. 'Are you having a sister hug…without me?'

'Get over here.' Jasmine beckoned and Lydia didn't need to be told twice, bouncing towards them with her boundless energy, reminding Molly of one of the rabbits.

'Typical.' It was George, coming around the corner to find his five sisters all in some sort of weird hug-huddle. 'You girls. You always do this hugging thing. Well, I'm gonna get my own boy-hugging-huddle happening.' He turned and walked off down the side path towards the back yard.

'A boy-hugging-huddle? This I've got to see,' Stacey said and the sisters all followed their only brother towards the back garden, Molly bringing up the rear. She half expected to find George demanding the men all stand around and hug but, instead, she saw the back yard, perfectly decorated with fairy lights and white triangle-shaped bunting strung from the trees. There were even a few balloons filled with helium and tethered to lower branches.

'What's all this?' Molly asked, looking around because everyone else there—including Fletcher—seemed to know exactly what was going on.

'It's your wedding day!' It was Ty who shouted the answer, jumping up and down with excitement and clapping his hands.

Cora laughed at her son. 'Otherwise known as your renewal-of-vows day…or night, given that the sun is starting to set.'

'What? But I've got nothing to wear.'

'Oh, yes, you do.' Jasmine tugged at her hand. 'Come inside, sis. Everything's taken care of.'

'But…' Molly glanced at Fletcher over her

shoulder, half expecting some sort of support, but all she received was a kiss, blown to her. 'When did you plan all this?'

'It was Fletcher's idea.' Stacey led Molly down the hallway towards the bedroom. 'He wanted to wait until you'd finished all your exams but didn't want to stress you with having to plan any of it. So as you weren't available—'

'He turned to those who know you better than you know yourself.'

'Us!' Lydia provided Molly with the answer to the rhetorical question as they entered the bedroom. 'Look. We all helped pick the dress, even George.'

'He was so funny, Molly. Incredibly particular and thoughtful.' Cora spoke softly near Molly's ear.

'Well…I don't know what to say. I'm speechless.' She looked at her sisters, one by one, her heart swelling with love. 'Thank you. All of you.'

'You're more than welcome, but let's get you changed.'

'Wait a moment. What about Fletcher? What's he going to wear?'

'He's getting changed, too. Come on or we'll

run out of time.' Stacey was in organisational mode and there was no arguing with her when she was like this. And before Molly knew what was really going on, she was dressed in the most lovely cream-coloured raw satin dress, which came to just above her ankles. A pair of flat shoes matched the dress and Cora quickly put Molly's unruly curls into an easy up-do, securing it with a blue clip. Lydia handed Molly one of Letisha's old necklaces.

'This can be your something old and something borrowed,' Lydia stated as Stacey fixed the necklace into place. 'And the blue clip is your something blue and the dress is your something new. I made sure it was all organised.'

'Thank you, Lyds.' Molly hugged her sister close. 'All of you. Thank you.'

'You were so busy with exams,' Cora whispered near Molly's ear, 'that you probably didn't even guess.'

'I was wondering how you'd all managed to keep it a secret, especially you and Stace, but instead of trying to figure it all out, I'm going to just enjoy it.'

'As you're supposed to.' Cora pulled Molly to her feet and gave her a quick perusal. 'Perfect.'

'I'll go see how the boys are getting on,' Stacey remarked.

Soon, Molly was walking down the makeshift aisle, with George on her arm, 'giving her away', and heading towards Fletcher, who stood near the flowers Pierce had planted, smiling at her as though she were the most incredible, wonderful and perfect person in the world. Oh, how she loved him...with all her heart.

As they were already married, they didn't need a minister to officiate the ceremony and so, when they stood there, hand in hand, facing each other, their extended family around them, Molly and Fletcher declared their love for each other, promising to be there for each other—no matter what.

Afterwards, they celebrated in style, the fairy lights twinkling in the garden.

'Happy?' Fletcher asked as he handed her a glass of wine.

'More than I can ever remember being before.' She kissed her husband. 'I meant what I said in my vows.'

'I should hope so,' he joked.

'I do love you, more than words can express.'

'And I love you even more than that.' He nodded and hugged her close, the two of them in one corner of the garden as everyone else danced on the patio. 'This time we've got it. We're both ready. We're both in the same place.'

'I love that you tied the engagement ring to Katie's bear.'

'It was only right she be a part of our continued unity.'

'She *is* a part of us. For ever.' Molly looked up at the twinkling lights in the cloudless sky. Then she angled her head to one side, looking more intently at the stars.

'What are you looking at?' Fletcher asked her.

'Katie's star.'

'What?'

'I had a star named after her. Katie Wilton-Thompson. Just…over…there.' She pointed in the direction and Fletcher kissed the side of her neck, his arms still securely around her.

'What a lovely reminder of our beautiful girl. Her spirit, flying free amongst the stars, shining bright. For ever.'

'Just like us.' Molly put her drink down, then

turned in his arms. 'The two of us, together. For ever.'

Then she kissed the man she'd married so long ago, unable to believe how their topsy-turvy journey had brought them to this very point in time.

'Hey, you two!' Cora called. 'Stop cuddling and come and join in. This is *your* party.'

'Huh. What do you know?' Fletcher remarked as he kissed Molly once more. 'I finally got to cuddle you in the back yard.'

Molly laughed. 'Fletch. Promise you'll always make me laugh.'

'I promise, my love.'

And so they rejoined the party, dancing and laughing and having the most wonderful time, ending with Molly leading them all in a big conga line around the garden and through the house.

She fell onto the sofa, Cora and Stacey beside her.

'Thank you,' she said to them both. 'For everything.'

'That's what family's for,' they said in unison and the three of them laughed, all so very happy with the way their lives had turned out.

* * * * *